"Don't be as hell."

"I know I have an unsettling effect on some men, but it's been a long time since I used my sexual mojo on anyone. I'm a bit rusty."

She hadn't denied she was sexy. That made him respect her more. He liked that she accepted who she was and didn't try to pretend to be something she wasn't.

"You have my permission to practice on me," he said with a confident smile.

That was when she went on tiptoe and kissed him on the mouth. He had to admit, the move took him by surprise, but only for a second or two. Then it was on. For the longest time, he'd been wondering what it would feel like to kiss her. Now he knew. It was bliss itself. Her lips were full, juicy and sweeter than anything he'd ever experienced before. Her breath mingled with his and created an airborne aphrodisiac. Honestly, she tasted like heaven, a feast for a love-starved man who'd just been invited to an all-you-can-eat buffet. He had to force himself to hold back, because damn, the woman had made him wait forever for this kiss.

Dear Reader,

I never know how a couple is going to interact with one another until I start writing about them. Desiree and Decker truly surprised me. Decker brought out her playfulness. Desiree brought out his desire to be her hero and protector. I had fun getting to know them. I hope you will, too.

If you'd like to let me know what you think of their story, you can email me at Jani569432@aol.com, write me at PO Box 811, Mascotte, FL 34753-0811, look me up on Facebook, or send me a message via my website, janicesims.com.

Happy reading!

Janice

Thief OF MY *Heart*

JANICE SIMS

HARLEQUIN® KIMANI™ ROMANCE

Recycling programs for this product may not exist in your area.

ISBN-13: 978-0-373-86391-4

Thief of My Heart

For questions and comments about the quality of this book please contact us at CustomerService@Harlequin.com.

H HARLEQUIN®

Printed in U.S.A.

www.Harlequin.com

Janice Sims is the author of over thirty titles ranging from romance and romantic suspense to speculative fiction. She won an Emma Award for Favorite Heroine for her novel *Desert Heat*. She has also been nominated for a Career Achievement Award by *RT Book Reviews*, and her novel *Temptation's Song* was nominated for Best Kimani Romance Series in 2010 by *RT Book Reviews*. She lives in central Florida with her family.

Books by Janice Sims

Harlequin Kimani Romance

Temptation's Song
Temptation's Kiss
Dance of Temptation
A Little Holiday Temptation
Escape with Me
This Winter Night
Safe in My Arms
Thief of My Heart

Visit the Author Profile page
at Harlequin.com for more titles

This one is for my cousin, Cathy Johnson.
Cathy, your enthusiasm for life has always inspired me.
Besides that, if you hadn't made me put down a book
I was reading (bookworm that I am) and go shopping
with you on that fateful Saturday many years ago,
I never would have met my husband!

Acknowledgments

Working with the staff at Harlequin is always a pleasure.
Rachel Burkot, my editor, helps to keep me focused.
Caroline Acebo keeps me on schedule. And a special
shout-out to the art department for a very cool cover!
Just look at it. The model is exactly how I pictured
Decker Riley as I was writing his story. The background
and the couch he's sitting on are nice, too. :o)

Chapter 1

Decker Riley strode into the busy sports bar in downtown Raleigh, North Carolina, and looked around. Six-three and fit, he rolled his shoulders in an attempt to shake off the stresses of the day. His dark gray eyes scoped out the ladies in the establishment. A couple of beauties showed some interest. He smiled, they smiled back. *Maybe next time,* he told himself as he continued walking.

Suddenly he heard "Decker, over here!" from across the room. It was his cousin, Colton Riley, gesturing for him to join him. Decker smiled as he made his way through the crowd of Friday night revelers. It had been a few months since he, Colton, Juan and Will had gotten together. As he got closer, he saw that they had gone home after work and changed into casual clothes while he still had on his suit slacks and shirt. He'd left his tie and jacket in the car. Each of his three closest friends was married now, and things had changed between them. They had new responsibilities that didn't include hitting the clubs with their pals, or doing anything remotely fun like the way they used to, in his opinion. Sometimes Decker felt it was only a matter of time before they stopped making an effort to get together at all.

He sighed. That was probably his general dissatisfaction with life talking. Some part of him wanted what they had: a solid, loving relationship with a woman. He was thirty-four and had never been that lucky.

It was March, and March Madness was in full swing. The big-screen TVs at both ends of the huge room featured college basketball teams warring for a place in the NCAA's Final Four.

"What'd I miss?" Decker asked as he sat down at the table and accepted a mug of beer from Colton.

"Kentucky just kicked Michigan's butt," Juan Medina, a Mexican-American in his late twenties, said with a pained expression on his face. Decker knew that Juan was a fan of the Michigan Wolverines.

"Sorry, man," he said. "Maybe next year."

"Where've you been?" Colton asked as he moved the platter of chicken wings closer to him so he could partake of what was left.

"Tough day in court," Decker said, reaching for a boneless wing. He popped it into his mouth and chewed, relishing the spicy morsel. "So, how's life been treating you guys? Wives still got you whipped?"

They all laughed with the ease of friends who mercilessly teased each other on a regular basis. "You wish you were whipped like us," Colton said, gray eyes knowing.

Decker winced inwardly. His cousin had hit the nail on the head. "I'm perfectly happy dating different beautiful women every week. I'm not ready to have a ring put through my nose."

"That depends on who's putting the ring in it, my friend," Will Simpson, a tall African-American in his early thirties, said. "I bet if Desiree Gaines offered you a ring, you'd gladly let her put it in and lead you around by the nose."

"Don't mention that woman's name," Decker said defensively. "She's my one failure. She broke my perfect record."

"Let's keep this in perspective," his cousin said. "Desiree is an angel compared to the woman whose name we *really* dare not mention out of respect for your stomped-on heart."

"We're not going there," Juan said, grinning. "Back to Desiree. Come on, man. She crushed your record! Not only will she not go out with you, she won't even accept your flowers. How many times has she sent your flowers back now, ten, twenty times?"

"I'm wearing her down," Decker claimed with more bravado than he felt. "No one can resist this forever." He pointed to his face and preened, which only elicited groans of disgust from his less than appreciative audience.

"Maybe you're going about it the wrong way," Will suggested. He inclined his bald head in the direction of a group of young women gathered around the bar, chatting and giggling. "What do you see when you look at a pretty woman?"

Decker hesitated because Will tended to be a philosopher. He asked harmless-sounding questions, but he was rarely satisfied with simple answers. "Is this a trick question? What am I supposed to see, Will? I see an attractive face and body."

"Then you're not looking deeply enough," said Will. "Every woman has a distinct personality. You can't use the same old methods of seduction on every one of them. Desiree doesn't respond to a player. So you've got to figure out what she wants and give it to her."

Decker looked at Will and shook his head in exasperation. "What do you think I've been trying to do?"

"Get her into bed," Colton deadpanned.

"Eventually, yeah," Decker said, turning to face his cousin, who could have been his brother they looked so much alike. Both of them were tall, with reddish-brown skin, dark brown hair shorn close to well-shaped heads and the Riley gray eyes. "But I really care about her. Would I still be trying to get her to go out with me after almost two years if I didn't care?"

"I don't know," Colton said. "Maybe it irks you

that she's holding out, and now it's become important to you because you can't bear to lose. You've never been a good loser, Decker."

"I know you're married to her sister, but could you be on my side in this?" Decker asked plaintively. "I'm beginning to think it's your opinion that I'm not good enough for your sister-in-law!"

"Uh-oh," Will said in anticipation of a fight erupting between the cousins. "Keep the comments civil, fellas."

"It's not a question of your not being good enough for Desiree," Colton said levelly. "I know you're a decent man. But Desiree doesn't, and you're not giving her the room to observe you and come to that conclusion on her own. My advice is to quit sending her flowers and quit calling her altogether."

Decker frowned. "Did she tell you to talk to me? Is that it?"

Colton shook his head and sighed impatiently. "No, no one asked me to talk to you. But I'm doing it anyway. Leave her alone and let her miss you, Decker. Who knows? Maybe she'll miss the water when the well runs dry. Let's face it, at this point she's taking your attention for granted. Take it away, and see what happens."

Decker let Colton's words sink in. His cousin could be right. He had tried everything in his considerable arsenal to get Desiree to go out with him. Cards, flowers, emails and numerous messages left on her answering machine. And the only explanation he could get out of her as to why she wouldn't go out with him was the fact that she'd been in love once and her fiancé had died. She was, in essence, still in love with a man who had been dead for ten years. How was he going to compete with that?

He smiled regrettably at his cousin and said, "I've tried everything else. I don't suppose taking your advice could hurt."

"Unless, of course, it backfires and she's happy that you're giving up," Juan joked.

"Man, why'd you have to go there?" Will asked. "Now you're gonna make him doubt himself even more than he already does."

"No, he's right," Decker said quickly. "There is the possibility that this will backfire. But at least I'll know for sure that she's never going to consider dating me, and then I can move on. That woman has had me in a holding position for too long. I haven't dated another woman in over a year because of her. I'm going to qualify for sainthood soon."

His friends got a good laugh out of that assertion, after which Colton said, "I don't think there's a chance of that happening." Then he gave his cousin a serious look. "So, what's your plan?"

Decker pursed his lips, thinking. "I'm going to send her one last bouquet tomorrow with a message that will state my case once and for all."

Colton smiled his agreement. "One last attempt, huh?"

Decker nodded. "And if she sends them back, I'm moving on."

There were solemn looks all around the table,

true friends sympathizing with the plight of one of their own having to suffer through a case of unrequited love.

"Women can be so heartless," Juan said, shaking his head sadly.

"We're the real romantics," Will said, just before downing the rest of his beer and burping.

"But you know what Adam said when God gave him Eve," Colton put in with a smile. "Thank you, Lord. She's way better than apples!"

"Amen!" Decker said, laughing.

"Desiree, will you slow down?" Lauren Gaines-Riley complained loudly as she and her sisters jogged in a Raleigh park on Saturday morning.

Desiree glanced back at her older sister and grinned. "Nobody told you to party all night with Colton."

The day was bright and clear, the temperature in the low sixties. Lauren squinted at the sun before saying, "If you're going to party with anyone all night long, it should be your husband."

Desiree and her sisters got together every Saturday morning to exercise and catch up with each other's lives. Desiree, thirty-one, was single and a psychologist with a private practice. Lauren, thirty-three, was an architect. She was married and had a small son. The baby of the family, Meghan, twenty-seven, was single and a history instructor at a local university. The only sisters missing were Mina, twenty-nine, who ran a lodge near the Great Smoky

Mountains, several hundred miles away, and Petra, thirty-two, a zoologist presently studying the Great Apes in Central Africa.

Desiree laughed. She observed the puffiness of Lauren's eyes and the haphazard way she'd piled her thick black hair atop her head this morning. Lauren was usually put together for every occasion. "Yes, but he could at least let you get your rest afterward. You look like you didn't sleep a wink."

"I'll have you know these dark circles under my eyes are well worth a sleepless night with my man," Lauren said, laughing, too.

"Let's not start talking about sex," Meghan protested. The shortest of the sisters at five-six, she had recently cut off her long black hair and now wore it in a sophisticated bob. "Let's talk about hair, as in do you like my haircut?"

"I was trying not to say anything," Lauren said, peering at her sister's haircut with a critical eye. "I hope you don't regret it like I did when I cut mine off a few years ago. Long hair can be more trouble to keep up, but it has so many more styling options. I didn't know what to do with my short hair."

"That's because you were so used to long hair," Desiree said. "I loved my short hair."

"Then why are you letting it grow out?" asked Lauren reasonably.

"Because I think I look more intelligent with longer hair," Desiree said.

Lauren laughed harder. "You have a doctorate in

psychology. What does hair length have to do with intelligence?"

"We look on the outside how we feel on the inside," Desiree said. "Haven't you ever wondered why everyone has their own sense of style? Everything we wear, how we style our hair, it all depends on how we feel about ourselves. I think I look smarter with my hair in a bun. That's how I wear it when I'm in session. Looking intelligent makes my clients more confident in my ability to help them."

Lauren sighed loudly. "Wearing your hair up has no effect on your ability to help your clients. Your dedication coupled with your education and your willingness to give of yourself to everyone who comes to you for help is what makes you a good psychologist, my dear sister!"

"We all have little behaviors we rely on to make it through the day," Desiree said. "You, for example, have a habit of rubbing your left earlobe when you're thinking hard about something."

"I do not!" Lauren cried, brown eyes sparkling with humor.

"Yes, you do," Meghan confirmed. She looked at Desiree. "What mannerisms do I have?"

Desiree grinned at her. "You have a habit of shaking your leg nervously when you're sitting at the dinner table. And I don't know if you've noticed this, but you tend not to close things after opening them. You leave drawers open, cabinet doors, closet doors. When we were living at home with Mom and Dad, I used to go behind you, closing things. It drove Mom mad, but I don't think she ever caught you at it."

Meghan laughed heartily. "No, you're wrong, I know I have that problem, but I still can't shake it. I'll go behind myself to this day and close things hours after I've left them open." She looked at her sister with admiration. "That's why you became a psychologist. You're very observant of people."

"That and the cute boy she wanted to meet, who happened to be taking Psychology 101 at the time," Lauren quipped.

Desiree frowned, remembering how she had fallen in love with Noel Alexander her freshman year while sitting behind him in Psychology 101. He was tall and well built with the most beautiful milk-chocolate skin and dark brown eyes. She had been so in awe of him, she couldn't bring herself to walk up to him and introduce herself. If they hadn't accidentally bumped into each other one day while entering their classroom, they would never have met. Once Noel looked into her eyes, sparks flew and they were inseparable from that day forward.

"Why'd you have to bring him up?" she asked Lauren irritably. "I'm trying to forget I ever knew that creep."

Desiree picked up her pace. But her older sister was soon at her side again.

"You need to talk about it," Lauren said.

She and Meghan flanked Desiree.

Desiree sighed deeply and rolled her eyes. "I already told you two what happened."

"Yes, but it's been over a week now, and you haven't said how it makes you feel," Meghan said gently. "Finding out the man you loved, a man you idolized, cheated on you, must make you feel something!"

"And the way his mother just blurted it out in the middle of the cemetery like that," Lauren put in. "After ten years of keeping his son a secret! Come on, Desi, that must have pissed you off."

"Of course it pissed me off," Desiree said angrily. "What really irks me about it is I don't believe she would have told me at all if Noel Jr. hadn't been with her, and I immediately saw the resemblance between him and Noel. I think it was the look in my eyes that made her spill her guts. But what am I supposed to do about it, go cuss out a dead man?"

"Why not?" Lauren asked reasonably. "We'll go with you and make a party of it. We'll go at midnight and burn candles on his grave. And after you're finished cussing him out, we'll toast your new beginning with champagne."

"So that's it," Desi said, looking at Lauren suspiciously. "You think this is going to throw me into a depression."

"You did have that man on a pedestal for ten years," Meghan reminded her. "Whenever some other guy got too close to you, you would whip him out as the perfect example of fidelity and true love. No other man could compare to him. Now that you know he wasn't perfect, you must be regretting those lost years."

"Damn right I regret them. But I can't blame Noel for that. I was the one who chose to hide behind him in order to avoid relationships. I understand that about me."

"Then why won't you give Decker a chance?" asked Lauren.

"Because dating Decker Riley is just asking for trouble," Desiree said. "That man is sex personified. Noel was good-looking, but he didn't compare to Decker. If Noel could rip my heart out with his behavior, Decker will eviscerate me."

"I never took you for a coward," Lauren said. Her expressive brown eyes held a challenge in them.

Desiree knew that look well. Her big sister had been goading her into action all her life. This time she was not going to take the bait. "Well, where he's concerned, I'm a coward!"

Then she sprinted ahead of her sisters. And since she was by far the fastest runner in the family, she left them in her dust.

Chapter 2

As was his habit, Decker personally went to the florist's to choose the flowers he wanted Desiree to receive. He picked a spring bouquet because whenever he saw her, she was always turned out in the most appealingly feminine way. And it had not escaped his notice the past two years that pink was her signature color. She wore it in deep shades. She wore it in paler shades. It complemented her coppery brown skin, making it appear more beautiful than it already was. He thought about all this as he was running the wilderness trail he frequented on weekends. It was only a short drive from his neighborhood, the wooded surroundings were calming and the air out here reminded him of the mountains, which he loved.

He glanced down at his watch. It was almost noon.

He was nearing the end of his run, and he could see the secluded parking area up ahead where he'd left the SUV. There were more cars there now than when he'd gotten here. He slowed his pace until he was walking, which allowed his heart rate to return to normal before it would be time to get into his car and drive home. As he walked to the SUV, he wondered what Desiree had thought when she read the card. Would she think he was giving her an ultimatum? If so, that hadn't been his goal. He had just wanted her to know he cared for her, but he also knew when to throw in the towel. Now the ball was in her court.

Stoicism aside, though, he truly hoped she would call him, as he'd requested. If only his appeal had gotten through to her.

When Desiree got home from the park, there was a beautiful bouquet of spring flowers on the foyer table. She paused only a moment to appreciate their beauty.

She didn't linger over them because she knew who they were from: Decker. She had nothing against Decker, but Noel's infidelity was still too fresh in her mind for her to take any pleasure from them, or the sweet sentiments he invariably included in his notes. She resolved to ignore Decker Riley. Refused to even read the note. Then she headed to the kitchen for a bottle of water. Mrs. Neale, her housekeeper, had left a message for her on the dry-erase board on the wall next to the fridge. "Accepted flower delivery for you. Have you got a new beau?"

Desiree laughed at Mrs. Neale's comment. Honestly, why was everybody so eager to see her with a man? First her sisters, now Mrs. Neale. She was perfectly fine by herself. All she needed was to stay so busy with work and physical activities that she wouldn't have time to obsess about Noel, or dream about Decker's sexy gray eyes.

She was looking forward to her karate work-out with John next week. That usually helped to calm her and focus her thoughts.

"I'm older than you, so go easy on me," John Tanaka complained as Desiree's foot came a bit too close to his head while they were practicing karate in his basement. The room had been transformed into a large space for exercising. Atop the wooden floor was a thick rubber mat, and it was on this surface that they were going through their paces, each of them barefoot and attired in a gi, the lightweight two-piece garment common to martial arts, with black belts tied around their waists.

They faced each other again, in fighting stances, bouncing on the balls of their feet, each trying to figure out the other's weaknesses. In the past hour they'd worked up quite a sweat.

"Sorry," Desiree said, not breaking her concentration. John was not only her sensei; he was her therapist. They'd met three years ago at a psychology conference, and in the course of their conversation, they'd learned they were both into karate. John had learned the discipline from his father and practiced the Japanese style of the martial arts. Desiree had wanted to learn from him, so she suggested they try a practice session. Once they got on the mat, they knew they were compatible. It was John who suggested they give each other free psychological sessions while they worked out, killing two birds with one stone. So while they worked out their physical bodies, they also worked out their emotional problems.

"What angers you more?" John asked as he circled her. "That he cheated on you, or that you were oblivious to it?"

"What angers me is that I trusted him implicitly," Desiree said. She watched him closely because John had catlike reflexes honed from years of karate. He was fifteen years her senior and had been brought up in the discipline, whereas she'd only been a student since she was seven. It was difficult to focus on what he might do next and talk about the recent revelations concerning Noel that had left her so shaken. "Then, too, I'm pissed off because I wasted ten years mourning a man who obviously didn't love me as much as he said he did. On top of that, he's been dead for nearly a decade, and he still came out of this better than I did. He has a wonderful son, John. The boy seemed so sweet. He's respectful and adores his grandmother. And what do I have? I'm still single, and I have no prospects whatsoever!"

John laughed derisively. For a moment, Desiree's feelings were hurt that he would ridicule her like this when she was pouring her heart out to him. But one look into his sly eyes, and she knew that he was just trying to get a rise out of her. He wanted her to fight for her life, not complain about it.

"Get real," John said. "I have no sympathy for a woman with a successful practice, family and friends who love her, who's stunning and has men tripping over themselves trying to get next to her, men whom she ignores because she's too scared to take another chance on love!" Then he cracked his neck, as he had a habit of doing when he was getting ready to strike like an angry viper. One day she would tell him that she had learned his many tells, but not today. She yelled, moved forward and flipped him, sending him sprawling onto his back on the thick exercise mat.

John landed hard. After he'd caught his breath, he looked up at her. "Are you done working off your anger yet? I'm going to be black-and-blue in the morning."

Desiree laughed and offered him a hand. John accepted it and got to his feet. He was around her height, five-eight, but he outweighed her by thirty pounds. Desiree often thought he looked like Keanu Reeves, with his dark, longish hair, now sprinkled with silver, dark brown eyes and olive skin.

He looked into her eyes now, his own lit with humor. "At the risk of more bruises, I'm going to say something to you, Desi."

Desiree smiled. "Your observations are always appreciated, Sensei." She bowed respectfully.

"Call the hot lawyer who's been pursuing you.

Have a torrid affair. You've got ten years of pent-up sexual energy that needs to be expended."

Desiree grinned. "Is that your professional advice?"

John smiled. "No, it's the advice of a dear friend."

They began walking to the back of the room, where Desiree had left her belongings on a bench. "Maybe I will. He sent me a beautiful bouquet of spring flowers last Saturday."

John's eyebrows arched with curiosity. "Did you send them back?"

"No, I kept them." Desiree suddenly realized that she had neglected to phone Decker and thank him for the flowers. Not only that, but she hadn't read his card yet, which was still somewhere in the bottom of her shoulder bag.

"Oh, my God, I feel terrible. I didn't even call to thank him for the flowers. I've never forgotten to thank him before. It slipped my mind!" She quickly grabbed her shoulder bag and a fresh towel she'd brought with her from the bench. "I've gotta go. Thanks for the workout, Sensei! Give my best to Evan." She bent and slipped on her sneakers, quickly tying the laces.

John's eyes softened at the thought of his long-time partner. "Can I tell him you're going to call the hot lawyer?"

"Yeah," Desiree said as she ran up the basement stairs. "But tell him not to get his hopes up because the hot lawyer might not even accept my call after I waited a week to thank him for the flowers."

"Oh, I wouldn't worry about that," John said confidently.

Chapter 3

The first thing Desiree did when she got to her car that Monday evening after her workout with John was to lean against it and dig in her shoulder bag for Decker's card. She felt bad about not calling him before now. Even when she rejected his flowers, she always phoned to thank him for the thought, after which he'd make a joke about it and they'd end up laughing together before ending the call. She made sure he knew it wasn't because she disliked him that she refused to go out with him. It was because he wasn't her type. Plus, there was the fact that they were related by marriage. She couldn't behave stand-offish with him because she saw him at all sorts of family functions. She didn't ignore him, or turn and leave the room when he entered. She was always civil and kind. The truth was, if not for the fact that he had a reputation for being a ladies' man, he might actually be her type. He was good at his job, devoted to family and friends, to say nothing of being a total hottie. She did have eyes!

She finally found the card and removed it from its tiny envelope. She immediately recognized Decker's expressive cursive writing and smiled. The message read "Desi, I know when to cut my losses. If I don't hear from you after you receive these flowers, I'll know you're never going to give me the chance to love you the way you deserve to be loved. Yet I'm still hoping to be yours someday, Decker."

Suddenly weak in the knees, Desiree leaned heavily against the car door, her gaze lingering on the note. She didn't know why she felt like this: happy and sad at the same time. Decker had never written anything so heartfelt on his cards before. The messages usually consisted of things like "Go out with me already" or "How about dinner tomorrow night?" Once he'd written "Hello from your friendly neighborhood stalker."

Standing there in John's driveway, she realized that Decker might be thinking things were over between them for good since she hadn't bothered to phone him. That must have been why he'd written that if he didn't hear from her, he would know she didn't want anything to do with him and would give up.

She was torn. Did she really want him to give up on her? To be honest, she had gotten some kind of weird satisfaction out of having a gorgeous man pursuing her. Flattery wasn't the half of it. Decker Riley provided the closest thing she'd had in her life that could be construed as a relationship with a man. John was right: she was scared to take another chance on love. Decker had been safe because she could hold him at bay.

Did she have the courage to call him and ask him out? If she didn't, what did that make her, a pseudo-psychologist? How could she help anyone else when she couldn't even overcome her own shortcomings? How could she advise anyone else about life when her own was so messed up?

She slipped the card back into her shoulder bag and got behind the wheel of the SUV. Picking up her cell phone, she ran a finger across the touch screen and selected Decker's cell phone number.

He answered after three rings. "Desiree?" He sounded tentative, as though he was unsure as to why she'd phoned him.

"Do you have a moment?" she asked softly.

"I'm home," he said. "You can have all the time you need."

"Thank you for the flowers."

He sighed. "It's been a week. I thought you weren't going to call." He didn't sound upset, though, just wary.

"I got sidetracked. I'll tell you about it sometime."

"You promise?"

"Yes, maybe over dinner?"

"You mean it?"

"Yes, Decker," she said with a short laugh. "I mean it. I know it's been a long time coming, but I'd like to see where a date with you will lead. Do you accept the challenge?"

He laughed, too. "Hell, yeah, I accept! I know exactly where I want to take you for dinner."

"Where is that?" she asked, her tone entirely too expectant for her comfort. She didn't want to sound overly eager.

"Don't you worry about where," said Decker. "Just tell me which night you're available, the time to be at your place and leave the rest to me. Are you game?"

Desiree was grinning now. This could be fun, a bit of spontaneity in her well-ordered life. "All right, Friday night at eight."

"I'll be there, beautiful. Wear your dancing shoes."

"You dance?"

"Of course I dance. All Riley men dance."

"What about Riley women?"

"Who do you think teach the Riley men?"

She laughed delightedly. "Then your mom taught you to dance?"

"She started when I was five years old. She told me all Southern gentlemen should know how to conduct themselves on the dance floor. She's very old-school."

Desiree had met his mother, June, on several occasions and liked her. She was always kind to her and, like her son, had a killer sense of humor. But she didn't strike her as old-school. She dressed beautifully in the latest designer fashions and drove a sports car, fast.

She laughed at his assertion. "Your mom's ultra-modern, and you know it."

"That she is," Decker admitted. "Deep down, though, she's traditional. She's getting very impatient with me."

"About?"

"Bringing some nice girl home to meet her and Dad," Decker said. "She likes *you*."

"I like her, too, but let's not talk about that until after the first date, okay?"

Decker laughed. "I'm getting a little ahead of myself, huh?"

"A little," Desiree said with a smile.

"I can hear a smile in your voice," Decker said. "You're not turned off by the thought. I'll take that. See you Friday night. Do you like Italian food?"

"Love it. Should I wear something casual or dressy?" Desiree asked before he could hang up.

"Let's keep it casual for the first date," Decker said.

"Okay," Desiree returned. "And Decker?"

"Yes?" he asked. His voice was so deep and sexy that Desiree could have sworn her toes were curling.

"Thanks for being so understanding about my not phoning sooner."

"You're welcome," was all he said, and they ended the call.

Desiree sat in her car for a moment, smiling. That hadn't turned out the way she had anticipated. She had believed she was making the call to prove to herself that she wasn't a coward and could go forward with her life. But once she heard Decker's voice, something inside her melted. She began to genuinely look forward to going out with him and getting to know him better than the "surface Decker" she had known for the past two years. She couldn't wait until Friday night.

Decker stood for a moment in his chef's kitchen, looking dumbly at the cordless phone in his hand before putting it back in its cradle. He couldn't believe Desiree had suddenly had a change of heart and decided to give them a chance. Now he was dying to know why. What had made her do it?

Maybe she'd confided in her sister. He picked up the phone again and dialed Colton's cell. Colton didn't answer. When it went to voice mail, Decker hung up. He wanted to speak directly to his cousin. He dialed Colton and Lauren's home number.

Lauren answered, and she sounded a bit breathless. "Decker, what's up?"

"Lauren, have you spoken with Desiree lately?"

"We briefly chatted earlier today," Lauren said. And then she said something softly to someone who was evidently with her at the moment. Decker couldn't make out what she'd said.

The next voice he heard was Colton's. "Look, Decker, unless this is a life-or-death situation, we'll call you back later. We're busy, if you know what I mean."

"Sorry," Decker said, chuckling. "I just wanted to let you know your plan worked. Desiree just phoned me. We're going out Friday night."

"What!" Decker heard Lauren shout. Then she apparently took the phone from her husband. "When did this happen?" She sounded delighted, which made Decker grin even wider.

"A few minutes ago," Decker said. "Did she mention anything to you about why she changed her mind about me?"

"No," Lauren said, her tone puzzled. "I'm as surprised as you are, but I'm happy to hear it." She paused. "She *has* gone through something traumatic recently, though, so maybe that had something to do with her sudden turnaround. But that, I'm afraid, is something she'll have to tell you about herself."

Decker was instantly concerned for Desiree. Something traumatic, Lauren had said. Now his curiosity was doubly engaged. But he didn't press Lauren. "Okay," he said. "I'll let you get back to what you were doing. Thanks, Lauren."

"Congrats," Lauren said. "Treat her like the queen she is!"

"You know I will," he said with a smile.

After he'd hung up, he sat on a stool at the island in the kitchen, his brow furrowed by a frown. His heart ached with the knowledge that Desiree was in emotional pain right now, and he could do nothing to lessen it.

He got up and went to the fridge to get ingredients for a quick beef strip stir-fry. Cooking always calmed him and helped him think. Ironically, it was his father and not his mother who'd given him his appreciation of cooking. Thaddeus Riley, whom everyone called Tad, told his son that knowing how to cook upped a man's chances of landing the right woman. He swore that was how he'd won June's heart.

As he chopped fresh vegetables at the counter, he thought about the first time he'd seen Desiree. The occasion had been a sad one. It was at his uncle Frank's funeral. The service had ended, and those attending were spilling out of the church, preparing to go to the cemetery for the interment. He'd spotted a tall, shapely woman in a dark skirt suit standing in the middle of the crowd looking around as if she'd misplaced someone. He'd been instantly drawn to her, and before he knew it he was standing in front of her, offering to help her find whomever she had lost.

Desiree Gaines had creamy golden-brown skin, and when she looked up at him, she blushed noticeably. Her eyes were the color of honey, big, wide-spaced and thickly lashed. He remembered that when his gaze had fallen on her mouth, his heart skipped a beat. Those full lips looked so inviting, he had sighed inwardly when she parted them and said, "I'm all right, thank you. I see my sister just a little ahead of me over there." She had pointed at a woman who favored her but was a couple of inches taller.

Decker knew he was running out of time at that point and had started talking fast. "Look, I know this is going to sound strange at a funeral, but you are the most beautiful creature I've ever seen, and having just found you, I don't want to lose you again." He reached into his jacket pocket, retrieved one of his cards and pressed it into her palm. He had felt her reluctance to let him do that. She withdrew her hand from his at the first opportunity. But Decker was determined not to let that be the last time they met.

He held up his hands to show that he meant her no harm, and said, while backing away, "I've got to go. They're waiting on me so we can go on to the cemetery, but call me, please. You won't regret it."

Desiree had merely smiled at him with a somewhat doubtful expression on her beautiful face. He had never expected to see her again. But less than two hours later, she had shown up at his aunt Veronica's house with her sister, Lauren. Decker only learned later that Lauren and Colton were an item by then. He just thanked his lucky stars that he'd gotten another chance to speak with Desiree.

He laughed now. *Not that it got me anywhere,* he thought. *She still made me wait two years.*

"How do you feel about gaining five more pounds?" Desiree asked Madison Samuelson, age fifteen, who was seeing her for treatment for the psychological effects of anorexia nervosa.

It was Tuesday afternoon, and they were in her office, decorated to put her clients at ease. The furnishings were modern pieces done in expensive brown leather. The pillows, rugs and draperies were in earth tones, and the hardwood floor was light pine.

The windows were double-paned to prevent outside noises from intruding.

Desiree sat in a chair with her legs crossed opposite Madison, who sat on the couch with her legs tucked underneath her. She had medium brown skin and big light brown eyes. Her shoulder-length hair was in braids, and she invariably wore a scarf over it, which made Desiree wonder why she covered her head. Was she hiding something? Sometimes girls who had issues such as Madison's inflicted pain on themselves by pulling their hair out at the roots, cutting themselves, anything that made them forget their mental pain for a moment.

"I feel good!" Madison cried, eyes looking anywhere but directly at Desiree. Desiree recognized this as avoidance. Madison wasn't here willingly. Her parents had insisted she come to these sessions, and she probably didn't think they were doing any good. When Desiree had first seen Madison, who was five-five, she had weighed only eighty pounds. Today she weighed a hundred and five pounds, and her skin, hair, teeth, everything about her physical body looked much healthier. But Desiree was still concerned that so far what they'd been able to accomplish was only a Band-Aid on the surface of what was a much deeper cut to Madison's psyche.

They still hadn't gotten to the root of the problem. Why Madison had started starving herself. Madison would only say some girls at school had told her she looked fat, and she'd wanted to fit in, so she had started eating less. Soon eating less had turned into eating practically nothing in a twenty-four-hour period. She'd been rushed to the hospital with heart failure before her parents realized how far gone she was.

Desiree suspected Madison harbored resentment for her parents because they hadn't noticed her going downhill sooner. However, Madison had never said a word against her parents. Her comments, in fact, were always positive, as if giving upbeat responses would get her out of therapy that much quicker.

Until now, Desiree hadn't wanted to put any pressure on Madison, believing that the girl would respond to simply having someone to listen to her grievances. However, Madison was pretending she didn't have anything to complain about.

Therefore Desiree would have to take a different approach to the girl's treatment: anger. Some people had to get angry before they could move on to the next level.

"Madison," Desiree said, looking at the girl's face, which was impassive. "How do you suppose your parents missed the fact that you were practically skin and bones before they noticed you needed help?"

Madison swung her legs off the couch and sat up, staring at Desiree with her mouth agape and eyes wide. She gasped and closed her mouth. She looked at Desiree with one eyebrow raised higher than the other, as if to say, "Oh, no, you didn't go there!"

Desiree fought to keep her facial expression neutral because she was delighted that she'd gotten a rise out of the girl. There was actually some spunk left in her!

Madison looked her straight in the eye and said, "Because they were too busy working, chasing the mighty dollar, to see that I was dying."

"And what were *you* doing?" Desiree asked. "Wearing baggy clothes to hide your body? Pretending to eat at the dinner table, but really throwing food away? Are you saying you had nothing to do with their complacency, their blindness, where your condition was concerned, Madison?"

"Oh, yeah, sure, I was sneaky about things, but they should have still noticed! I needed them, and they weren't there. The only thing they were interested in was that my grades were good and I was on schedule for the perfect life they had planned for me. A 4.0 grade point average, my mother's alma mater, Howard University, becoming a lawyer like both of them, those were the things they cared about. Not the fact that I was being bullied at school, told I was fat and ugly and that no boy would want to be seen with me."

"Did you try to talk to them about what was going on at school?"

"Yeah," Madison said with a grimace. "They just said it was a part of growing up and to suck it up. It would give me character."

"So you turned your rage inward and started punishing yourself," Desiree said. "You started starving yourself because you felt like no one cared about you?"

Madison's eyes brightened. She let out a huge sigh and returned to her more relaxed position on the couch with her feet tucked under her. Looking at Desiree with a smile on her face, she said, "After six months, you finally figured me out. I was beginning to lose hope. Not that I didn't get a big kick out of knowing my parents have to pay a huge fee to you so that I can come here and sulk once a week. But really, Doctor D, I figured you were as full of crap as my parents. But you really know your stuff."

Desiree smiled at her. "Why do I feel as though you're just telling me what I want to hear?" She leaned forward, keeping her gaze on Madison's. "That may be part of it. But I don't think you're being entirely truthful with me. Why don't you take off that scarf you have on? And then we can get down to the real reason you wanted to die, Madison."

"No," Madison said adamantly. Her eyes narrowed. Her jaw clenched, and her bottom lip protruded. Desiree thought she looked as if she would rather fight her than take that scarf off.

"Have you replaced one bad habit with another?" Desiree asked. "You have everyone watching you like a hawk, making sure you're eating right and keeping it down. But maybe when you're alone in your room, you do something else to punish yourself."

Madison got to her feet and yelled down into Desiree's face, "I don't have to do anything I don't want to do. And you can't make me, you nosy bitch!"

Desiree sat in her chair and calmly looked up at

Madison. "That's right, I'm a nosy bitch. For six months you've sat on that couch lying to me, and I'm tired of it. If you don't think you're worth saving, why should I? If you don't want to fight for your life, why should I?" Now she stood, her eyes never leaving Madison's face. "You want to know a secret, Madison? We are born into this world alone, and we die alone. In between life and death, those of us who survive learn one valuable lesson—we've got to love ourselves. We can't count on others to love us, because human beings are selfish. They live in their own worlds. You've got to love yourself, Madison. You've got to care about yourself if no one else does. And you've got to fight to stay alive! Now, you can leave here today, resenting your parents, parents who love you, no matter how much you think they don't, and thinking of *me* as that nosy bitch who has wasted your valuable time, or you can choose to live, take care of yourself, be strong and accept the fact that no one can do it for you. I'm not going to waste any more of your parents' money on sessions with you, Madison. If you want to be rid of me, you are rid of me. Don't come back here." She pointed to the door. "Now get out. The big bad world is waiting for you. Either it will eat you up, or you'll learn to fight back and choose life, your choice!"

Madison was looking at her as though she'd lost her mind. She angrily snatched her shoulder bag off the couch and began walking toward the door. "I'm going to tell my parents how you talked to me, and they're going to sue your ass."

"That's fine. Your mother's just outside that door in the waiting room," Desiree said, undaunted. "Goodbye, Madison."

For a moment, Madison stood frozen, staring at her; then her mouth began trembling, and she started crying. She looked at Desiree helplessly, tears soaking her cheeks. "I'm scared," she said pitifully. In a defeated gesture, she dropped her shoulder bag back onto the couch and reached up to remove the scarf. Desiree gasped when she saw the many bald spots on the girl's scalp. She had to force herself to stand there, when her gut reaction was to immediately comfort Madison. Meanwhile the brave teen struggled to find her next words. "He said no one would ever believe me if I told," Madison finally said.

"He?" Desiree gently coaxed.

"Mr. Sawyer, my math teacher. I'm his classroom aide. His class is the last of the day, and I stay late and help him collect papers to grade, clean the classroom, that kind of thing. It started with warm hugs, and then one day he just grabbed me. I didn't know what to do. I didn't do that. I knew girls who did, but I didn't do that. Now I'm one of them. I'm one of those girls who let boys do things to them. I let him, and I keep letting him."

Desiree was across the room and pulling Madison into her arms in a flash. She had known there was more to Madison's suffering, but she had not imagined anything this horrible.

"Everything's going to start getting better from this moment," she promised Madison as she rocked the girl in her arms. "He's never going to touch you again. He's never going to touch any child again."

Madison wept, and Desiree got madder. "Baby girl, men like Sawyer not only molest young girls' bodies, but they manipulate them and prey on their minds. But you can get the power that he took from you back by making sure that he's punished for what he did to you. You're not the victim here. You're the strong one."

She walked over to her desk with Madison still in her arms and pressed the intercom on her phone. When her assistant, Mellie, answered, she said, "Mellie, tell Mrs. Samuelson to get in here now."

Chapter 4

Decker was having a good week. With the aid of a crack private investigation team that worked for his firm, he'd successfully represented a construction company owner accused of killing his business rival. The investigators had uncovered evidence the police had overlooked, proving that Decker's client had been set up by the wife of his rival who sought not only to get rid of her husband and collect the insurance money, but to let someone else take the blame for her crime.

It was with much satisfaction, on Friday afternoon, that Decker heard the judge proclaim, "Case dismissed!"

Decker turned to his client and shook his hand. The poor man appeared almost faint with relief. He enthusiastically pumped Decker's hand. "I can't thank you enough!" he cried, with tears of happiness in his eyes.

"My pleasure," Decker assured him. "Now go hug your wife."

His wife was waiting just behind them. Decker picked up his briefcase and he and his paralegal, Mike Lofton, left the courtroom. On the way down the courthouse steps, his cell phone rang. It was his administrative assistant, Kym Johnson. "Sir, I've got mayoral candidate Todd Pratt on the other line. He's been arrested on corruption charges. He wants you to represent him."

"Not another corrupt politician," Decker complained. Last year he'd represented a former state senator accused of accepting bribes. Turned out the senator had lied through his teeth when he said he was innocent, and all it took was a good attorney to convince the jury of it. Well, Decker had fought valiantly while evidence of the senator's guilt had piled up. The senator had gone to prison. After that Decker vowed to stay clear of politicians. "Tell him he'll have to get himself another lawyer," Decker told Kym.

"Whatever you say, sir," said Kym.

Decker put his phone away and turned to Mike, an eager young man who was working as a paralegal while he studied for his law degree. "You know what, Mike," Decker said, looking up at the clear blue, late March sky, "why don't you take the rest of the day off? I think I'll head home."

Mike beamed. "Why, thank you, sir."

"Go have fun," Decker said. He was feeling mag-nanimous. An innocent man was free to go home with his loving wife. It was a beautiful spring day. Best of all, he was going to be seeing Desiree in a matter of hours.

He and Mike said their goodbyes and parted, going in opposite directions. Decker walked swiftly to the parking garage across the street. He couldn't wait to see Desiree.

They'd spoken over the phone a couple of times this past week but had not seen each other. When they were on the phone he'd ask her how she was doing, wanting her to open up to him and tell him what sort of traumatic experience she'd recently gone through. But he could tell from her tone that she'd wanted to keep things light between them. He'd then asked her about work, which she said she couldn't talk about much because of doctor/patient confiden-tiality. She would make vague references to her cli-ents like how she felt close to a breakthrough with one patient, or she felt she wasn't getting anywhere with another one, but never any mention of a spe-cific mental illness.

As a lawyer, he understood the need to keep priv-ileged information under wraps. He simply wanted her to share her life with him.

He tossed negative thoughts aside as he climbed into the SUV, drove out of the parking garage and headed home. He had a great night planned for them. He was taking her to his favorite Italian restaurant in downtown Raleigh. They served Tuscan-inspired Italian cuisine. The atmosphere was relaxed, just the sort of place he and Desiree could sit and talk, laugh a little, get to know each other better. Then they'd go to a little jazz club he knew where they could have a drink and dance the night away. It was Friday; they could stay out late. He would like nothing better than to see the sun rise with Desiree tomorrow morning. But he would take his cues from her. Whatever the lady wanted would be his pleasure to give her.

Desiree's doorbell rang at six that evening. She had been home only about thirty minutes and was preparing to take a long soak in the tub. She walked through her Mediterranean-style home, attired in a bathrobe, and looked through the peephole.

Her sisters stood on the portico, waving enthusiastically. She swung the door open, one hand on her hip. "What are you two doing here?"

Shaking her head in mock consternation as she strode inside, Lauren said to Meghan, "She hasn't had a date since God created the world, and she's asking what we're doing here."

"We're here to help you prepare for your date," Meghan said, holding up a bottle of champagne. "And to get you slightly drunk, so you'll relax and have a good time with Decker tonight."

Lauren closed and locked the door, and she and Meghan followed Desiree upstairs to her master bedroom, where she immediately began pulling clothes from Desiree's closet and placing them on the bed while Meghan popped the cork on the champagne. Meghan ran to the sink in the adjacent bathroom and let the residual foam spill from the bottle's mouth into the sink. Then she drank some of the delicious bubbly directly from the bottle.

"What, are you uncivilized?" Desiree cried. "Go downstairs and get some glasses, baby sister!"

Meghan laughed. "No, tonight you're going to drink from the bottle, choose something sexy to wear, something that'll make Decker's eyes pop out of his head, and you're going to stay out late and scandalize nosy Mrs. Brown next door when you drag yourself home just before sunrise." She shoved the bottle at Desiree. "Here, drink!"

Desiree took the champagne and drank a little. It was cold and dry, just the way she liked it. But the last thing she wanted to do was get a little intoxicated before going out with Decker.

Drinking made her lose her inhibitions. She needed her inhibitions with Decker because they were the only things that would help her maintain a sense of decorum around him tonight. All week she'd found herself daydreaming about him. She hadn't seen him in a while, not since the last family get-together at Colton and Lauren's house about three months ago. And she had no photographs with him in them. So she had to rely on memory to recall how devastatingly handsome he was. Because of this, each time she found herself face-to-face with him, she was stunned by how bad her memory was. He was always much more appealing in the flesh than in her imagination. The man was endowed with a powerful presence. She couldn't deny that. So staying sober seemed like a good idea right now. She dutifully handed the bottle back to Meghan and announced, "I'm going to take a bath."

"You do that," said Meghan, turning toward the walk-in closet where Lauren was riffling through Desiree's clothes.

Desiree got into the tub of warm, fragrant water, relaxed with her head against an inflated pillow and closed her eyes. She hoped her sisters would give her a few minutes of alone time, but that hope was instantly dashed when Lauren called from the closet, "Didn't Decker say tonight was casual? Do you own any jeans at all?"

Desiree sighed. "Not the jeans talk again. You know I don't wear jeans. I'm not a jeans girl. I wear slacks sometimes, but I don't like jeans."

"Are you human?" Meghan joked. "Who doesn't like jeans?"

"Have you ever tried to kick someone while wearing tight jeans?" Desiree asked. "You can't do it."

Lauren laughed. "So you don't wear jeans just in case you're attacked and you have to defend yourself? That's ridiculous. In that case, you don't wear long, tight skirts, either."

"I don't," Desiree confirmed.

"You still wear your Louboutin shoes," Lauren said realistically. "Those aren't exactly made for fighting."

"You can kick those off," Desiree said languidly.

"Now, would you please let me pretend I'm alone at an exclusive spa with no one around except the towel boy waiting with a warm towel for me when I get out of the tub?"

"Who does the towel boy look like in your fantasy?" Meghan asked, laughing. "In mine he looks like Idris Elba."

Before Desiree could reply, Lauren said, "Why not Leo?"

Meghan took a swig of champagne. "Honestly, that man is driving me to drink. I know he wants me. He looks at me like he could devour me. Yet he's got it in that thick head of his that he's too old for me, so he says we should just be friends. That's why I'm replacing him in my fantasies with Idris."

"You never know what's going to happen," Desiree said to Meghan. "I never dreamed I'd be going out with Decker, either, but here I am, preparing myself to be sniffed, possibly touched and generally, hopefully, adored by him."

"Oh, you don't have to hope too hard," Lauren informed her with a laugh. "That boy already adores you. I'm just hoping the fire that ignites between you two tonight doesn't burn down Raleigh."

Desiree laughed at that. "I've admittedly gone through a very long drought, but there will be no fire tonight. There may be some smoldering embers ignited, but no fire."

"Wait and see," Lauren said as if she knew what she was talking about. "You've never been alone with a Riley man before. There's something very sexy about those gray eyes of theirs, to say nothing of those tall, hard bodies. When God created them, he should have patted himself on the back for a job well done."

"I've resisted him for nearly two years," Desiree reminded her as she laid her head back on the pillow.

"No," Meghan said. "You didn't resist him, you avoided him. There's a difference. You never let yourself be in an intimate setting with him. You never allowed yourself to be vulnerable around him. There's a difference, as you'll find out tonight."

Lauren looked at Meghan with admiration. "For the youngest of the bunch, you're pretty smart."

"Thanks, sis," Meghan said.

Desiree sighed. "Will you two hens let me bathe in peace?"

Instead they joined her in the bathroom, where Lauren sat down on the lowered toilet seat and Meghan perched her bottom on the dirty clothes hamper.

"Should we go over what to talk about tonight, and what not to talk about?" Lauren teased Desiree. "Let's see…" She turned to Meghan, enlisting her help. "You can tell him about your childhood, and your education. No harm in that."

Meghan nodded in agreement. "But don't tell him you talk in your sleep. That can wait until the relationship progresses a little."

"And please don't tell him you sometimes wake up singing," Lauren advised. "That'll freak him out."

Desiree splashed water on her for that. "You know I have no control over that! I sing when I'm happy."

Lauren chuckled and got a towel from the shelf to wipe the bathwater from her face. "I'm just trying to be helpful." Her eyes sparkled with good humor. "You know we love you, and we want you to be happy. I *do* get a little satisfaction from the fact that we've been telling you all along to give him a chance."

"Yeah," said Meghan. "First impressions aren't always on the money."

"I know," Desiree said quietly. "Unfortunately it took being disillusioned by Noel to make me realize that if I could misjudge *him*, I could also have misjudged Decker. But the jury's still out on that one, okay? This is the first date."

"Okay, then," said Lauren, rising. "Come on, Meghan, let's go find something in that closet of hers that says, 'Take me.'"

They got up to leave the bathroom. Desiree laughed. "Make that something that says, 'You can kiss me good-night, if you want.' But there will be no 'taking me' tonight!"

Lauren and Meghan laughed uproariously as they left, Lauren pausing long enough to pull the bathroom door closed after her.

Desiree slid farther down in the tub. "Alone at last," she said with a relieved sigh.

Decker arrived at five till eight. Desiree had forced her sisters to leave half an hour earlier. They had wanted to wait and see her off with Decker, a suggestion that she instantly vetoed. She had also put the low-cut dress that Lauren had picked out for her to wear tonight back in the closet, and had chosen a more modest style.

When Decker rang the bell, she ran downstairs, purse and jacket in hand, and pulled open the door. His attention was drawn to something on the street, and when she opened the door his back was to her. He turned back around, smiling, and when he saw her, his smile broadened in appreciation. "Wow," he said softly, his eyes running the length of her in the simple deep purple sheath dress with a black leather belt and a pair of black leather high-heeled sandals.

Desiree self-consciously touched her shoulder-length wavy black hair, which she'd combed away from her heart-shaped face. "Too dressy?" she asked.

Decker shook his head. "It's not too anything," he breathed. "It's perfect. You look beautiful."

Desiree smiled her thanks. She stood a moment, taking him in. As she'd predicted, she wasn't prepared for the effects of Decker in the flesh. The moment she opened the door and saw him standing there, his broad back to her, the first thing she'd experienced was the wonderful scent wafting off him. It was a fresh, woodsy, utterly male smell that made her momentarily weak in the knees. Then he'd turned around and faced her, and the full onslaught of a square-jawed, clean-shaven chestnut-brown face, with deep-set gray eyes that seemed so incongruous, yet so right, caused her heartbeat to accelerate.

He looked wonderful in jeans, a short-sleeve shirt in cobalt blue, a black leather jacket and black Italian loafers. "You look great, too," she said, suddenly shy.

Smiling, Decker stepped forward and put her hand through his arm. "I hope you're hungry because the restaurant we're going to serves the best Italian food you'll ever taste."

Desiree smiled up at him and let him lead her outside. He pulled the door closed and made sure it was locked before turning back around and peering down at her. "I have to be honest with you. I'm nervous."

Desiree laughed shortly. "Why? We've known each other for some time now."

His handsome face scrunched up in a frown. "Now that I've got you to go out with me, I don't know if I can live up to your expectations."

Desiree stopped in her tracks at the end of the walk and looked up at him. "Before this night gets started, I want to put your mind at ease. I have no expectations, except to get to know you better." She reached up and gently touched his cheek. "So just relax, okay?"

Decker grasped the hand she'd touched him with and brought it to his mouth, kissing the palm. Desiree was shocked by how turned on she was just by the meeting of his lips with her palm.

Unless she was reading him wrong, when he raised his head, his gray eyes glittered with intense longing. The look left her slightly breathless and unbalanced. She covered her weakness with an equally weak joke: "I hope you're not taking me to a restaurant that serves tiny portions. I'm famished, and I'm not one of those women who eat like a bird."

Decker laughed, appearing more relaxed. "I've been watching you eat for a while now. I know you can put it away."

To which Desiree laughed, and took his hand. "Come on." And they left the house.

He helped her into the car, which was parked at the curb. Once she was in, he closed the door and quickly walked around to the driver side. Inside, he buckled up while she did the same; then he turned the key in the ignition and the car purred to life. John Legend's latest CD was in the player. He reached over and turned the volume down. "Are you a fan?" he asked as he smoothly pulled away from the curb.

Desiree sat back on the soft leather seat. "Yes, I like him, but I'm more of a blues girl."

"Like who?" Decker prodded.

"Lots of artists, from those who come from the Mississippi Delta school when they used mostly acoustic guitars, to Chicago-style blues where the electric guitar replaced the acoustic," she said. "I love B.B. King, John Lee Hooker, Buddy Guy, Etta James, Koko Taylor and newer blues artists like Gary Clark Jr., Robert Cray and Keb' Mo'."

"Funny, I wouldn't have pegged you for a blues lover," Decker said, smiling at her briefly before returning his attention to the road. "I figured you for a smooth jazz aficionado. Or a Justin Timberlake fan."

Desiree laughed softly. "Goes to show you shouldn't judge a book by its cover." She paused, looking at his profile in the dim light of the car. "That's the same mistake I made with you," she said.

She heard Decker's sharp intake of breath. She had probably shocked him by saying that.

He exhaled. Clearing his throat, he looked into her eyes for a moment without saying anything. Then he continued driving for a couple more minutes before quietly saying, "It means a lot to me that you would admit that."

"I can admit when I make a mistake," Desiree said, keeping her tone light even though she had filled up with emotion when she'd seen just how affected Decker had been by her confession.

She figured now was as good a time as any to tell him why she'd changed her mind about going out with him. "Do you remember me telling you about Noel Alexander, the man I was engaged to?"

He let out a nervous laugh. "How can I forget? It was the night I threw Colton a bachelor party at a strip club and some fool ran him down in the parking lot, almost killing him. That image isn't going to leave my mind anytime soon." He breathed deeply and exhaled. "But you comforted me at the hospital later that night."

"I could see that you were hurting," Desiree said softly.

"For me, it was the most hopeful night and the most disappointing where you were concerned," he said. "You were so kind to me, and then you told me why you could never be with me. You had known true love, and you wouldn't settle for less. And there

I was, drunk, smelling like a distillery, feeling guilty because my cousin was lying in a hospital bed. I knew I didn't stand a chance with you."

"It wasn't just you who didn't stand a chance," Desiree said. "No one did. I'd brainwashed myself into believing that I was precious to Noel and that he was committed to me when he died. But a couple of weeks ago I was visiting his grave, and his mother also happened to be visiting. With her was a young boy who looked remarkably like Noel. Same skin, eyes, nose, you name it. He was Noel all over again. Noel's mother asked the boy to go wait for her at the car, and then she told me that he was Noel's son. He'd been born a few months after his death. Even though Noel and I were engaged, he had a lover. So, you see, I'm not a great judge of character. I adored Noel. I planned to spend the rest of my life with him. But I turned *you* down because you struck me as a player, when you could've been the nicest man I'd ever meet. You could've been perfect for me, but I would never know that if I refused to give us a chance to find out."

"How are you coping with what you found out about Noel?" Decker asked, sounding stunned himself.

Desiree smiled. "I'm coping by eating too much ice cream, throwing myself into work, beating up my sparring partner, overexercising to make up for the ice cream and questioning every decision I ever made, that's how. I'm human and I'm hurting right now, but I'm also a mental health professional, and I know, realistically, that wallowing will not get me anywhere. Therefore I'm taking steps to get over the disappointment and get on with my life. So, here we are, on a date. Do you still want to date me?"

Decker's laugh this time was more relaxed. "This is priceless. I always knew you had a sense of humor, but I never suspected you might be a little nutty."

"We're all a little nutty, Decker. Didn't you know that?"

"I suspected as much," he said with slow smile.

Beside him, Desiree sighed softly. So far, her sisters were right: there might be a fire tonight, after all.

Chapter 5

The restaurant was on Main at North Hills. They were in time for their eight-thirty reservation, and were greeted at the entrance by a friendly hostess who knew Decker by sight. "Good evening, Mr. Riley. Welcome back."

"Thank you," said Decker with a smile, his hand on the small of Desiree's back. "We have a reservation."

"Yes, we're ready for you. Right this way," the hostess said with a warm smile. She led them to a secluded table in the back, just as Decker had requested when he phoned. He didn't want anything to take his attention away from Desiree tonight.

At the table, he pulled out Desiree's chair for her and sat down across from her. Then the hostess presented them with menus and said, "I'll send a waiter over. Enjoy your evening!"

"Thank you, I'm sure we will," Decker replied, his eyes on the beautiful woman sitting across from him. Desiree was busy hanging her jacket on the back of her chair, along with her shoulder bag. She looked up at him when she was done and smiled. "I like the ambience in here," she said.

Decker also liked the warm, welcoming vibe this restaurant had. The décor was modern Italian with scenes from Tuscany on the walls, gleaming hardwood floors, abundant greenery in the form of hanging plants and small trees in huge pots. The tables were covered in pristine white cloths, in the center of which candles glowed in long-stemmed glasses.

He watched Desiree as she read the menu. Her eyes were golden brown rimmed in dark brown with thick black lashes. Her sculpted black eyebrows gave her face a natural, fresh appearance that appealed to him.

She looked up and caught him watching her. "What do you suggest?"

Decker didn't even have to look at the menu. "I suggest the brushetta à la Romana as an appetizer. It's garlic toast, marinated tomatoes, mozzarella and olive oil. You're not lactose intolerant, are you?"

"No," Desiree said. "I like dairy."

"Good." He smiled. "They have a chocolate gelato that's to die for."

"Mmm, chocolate," said Desiree, her eyes dreamy.

"I can't resist a good chocolate dessert. I can't resist a good chocolate anything."

Decker guessed from her expression that she thought her comment might have been too suggestive. He couldn't resist saying, "Do I qualify?"

Desiree laughed and gave him a reproving look. "Behave yourself. You knew what I meant."

"Yes," he admitted, "but you blush so prettily."

The waiter arrived at that moment and asked if they'd like to order pre-dinner drinks. Desiree declined, as did Decker. "We'd just like to go ahead and order a bottle of wine with dinner," Decker said to him.

After they'd ordered and the waiter had gone, Decker said, "Earlier you mentioned a karate instructor. I'd heard from Colton that you and your sisters started taking karate when you were kids, but I didn't know you still practiced."

"Oh, yeah, I love it," Desiree said, meeting his eyes. "It's like therapy to me. It keeps me centered."

"What level have you achieved in it?" Decker asked, curious. He practiced kung fu and had earned a black belt when he was sixteen. He still studied, and, as Desiree apparently believed, he also thought the discipline helped to keep him together physically, mentally and spiritually.

"I'm a third-degree black belt," Desiree said without a hint of self-congratulation, which he noted with surprise.

"That's quite an accomplishment," he said. "Yet you stated it as if it's just an everyday occurrence."

"That's because it's nothing to brag about," Desiree said. "My being a black belt means no more than another woman being an accomplished baker. It's something you have to learn and keep doing until you're good at it. Lauren told me you're also into martial arts."

He nodded. "Kung fu, which I admit I got into as a kid because I loved Bruce Lee movies."

Desiree smiled. "I understand. I think I've seen every martial arts movie ever made, beginning with *Enter the Dragon*. Bruce Lee was so cool."

"The coolest," Decker agreed. "Okay, so we both like the martial arts. What else do you like to do?"

"I run," Desiree said. "I love the high it gives me."

"I run, too," Decker said. "See how much we have in common? What are your favorite books and movies?"

Desiree moistened her lips and wrinkled her nose. Decker noticed she had a habit of wrinkling her nose when she was thinking hard. "I'll go first," he offered. "I like science-fiction novels by writers like Isaac Asimov and Octavia Butler."

"I love *Kindred* by Octavia Butler," Desiree exclaimed.

"I must have read *Parable of the Sower* ten times," Decker said excitedly. "She could really make you get lost in her stories. It was sad when she passed away."

"Yes, she was one of the greats," Desiree agreed.

"And your favorite writers?" Decker asked.

"Walter Mosley, Dean Koontz, Margaret Johnson-

Hodge, Melanie Schuster, Toni Morrison, Barbara Kingsolver, Neil Gaiman, Colson Whitehead, Dorothy West, Zora Neale Hurston and on and on. I read every day. There's always a book on my nightstand. Often, I'll go to sleep with a book in my hand." She laughed. "That sounds pretty pitiful, doesn't it?"

"No," Decker assured her. "It sounds sweet. And you're not the only one sleeping with books nowadays."

The look she gave him was disbelieving. "You're not about to tell me that you've been without a woman in your bed for as long as I've been without a man in mine?"

"I don't know how long it's been for you," he said, eyes boring into hers. "But it's been quite a while for me."

"I haven't slept with anyone since Noel," Desiree stated flatly.

"Not that long," Decker admitted, smiling at her. "And why haven't you?"

"Because I have to be in love before I'll go to bed with anyone," Desiree said softly. "That's just the way I'm built, and I make no apologies for it."

"Then what do you do to satisfy the urge when it hits you?"

Desiree hesitated. "I can't believe we're talking about sex on our first date."

"Why shouldn't we? You're a mental health professional, as you said earlier," he reminded her. "We're adults. We should be able to talk about anything."

She sighed, and to his relief, let down her guard and answered his question with "I do what any red-blooded woman would do—distract myself. I stay extra busy, take cold showers, read too many books, watch movies with hot guys in them and dream and eat chocolate."

"That's pretty much what I do," Decker joked, "except for the part about watching movies with hot guys in them."

Desiree cocked her head to the side, watching him closely. "Decker, if you're not a player, why do you pretend to be?"

"Isn't it obvious?" he said. "I'm hiding behind the facade because I'm afraid of getting hurt again."

"Someone broke your heart?"

"No, she tore it from my chest and stomped on it for good measure." He tried to keep the bitterness from his tone, but failed.

"Would you like to talk about it?" Desiree asked. The expression on her face was so genuinely caring that Decker felt compelled to tell her anything she wanted to know. He resisted that impulse with every fiber of his being. Nothing, he felt, would derail this relationship more effectively before it could even get started than hearing what a fool he'd been over a woman who had tossed him aside like so much trash.

"I can't tell you who she is, because you know her. Pretty much everyone in Raleigh knows her."

Desiree leaned forward. "Isn't that exaggerating a little? How can everyone in Raleigh know her?"

The waiter arrived with their plates, saving Decker

from having to answer right away. He breathed an inward sigh of relief as they were served. He didn't want to talk about Yolanda tonight.

After the waiter had poured wine into their glasses, he left them to their meal. Decker smiled at Desiree and said, "Please, dig in."

Desiree picked up a piece of the garlic toast piled high with a mixture of marinated tomatoes, mozzarella and olive oil and bit into it. He knew instantly when the juxtaposition of flavors hit her taste buds because she softly moaned with pleasure. She smiled at Decker. "You were right, this is wonderful."

Decker smiled his satisfaction, and for the next few minutes they ate in silence. He was the first to speak again. He took a swallow of the white wine and cleared his throat. "You know, Desi, I made a promise to myself that if you ever decided to give me a chance, I would give you all of me, and not hold anything back. I want you to know everything about me, even the embarrassing stuff. So here goes—five years ago I was in love with a beautiful woman who I thought was perfect for me. She was smart, talented, down-to-earth, or so I thought, and we fit, you know, we were so compatible that I knew we were meant to be together forever. Then she got her big break. For years she had been trying to break into the movies. She majored in theater in college, moved to New York City upon graduation and worked in off-Broadway plays for several years. But one day, she got the call. A big director had seen her in a play and wanted her to audition for a major part in his next film. She auditioned, and she got it. She called me the same day and told me it was over between us because I didn't fit into her image of her life anymore. Fact is, she'd been dating a well-known actor for months, and he'd been the one who arranged the audition."

Before he'd stopped talking, he saw the spark of recognition in Desiree's eyes. She was smart. It hadn't taken her long to figure out to whom he was referring.

"You're talking about Yolanda Reynolds, aren't you?" she asked, eyes stretched in horror, to his dismay. Why did the thought of Yolanda horrify her?

She rose, her expression almost accusing as she grabbed her shoulder bag off the back of the chair and said, "Excuse me, I have to go to the ladies' room."

Then she hurried away. Dumbfounded, Decker sat watching her retreating back. He started to get up and follow her but thought better of it and remained sitting. She obviously wanted some alone time, or she wouldn't have sought refuge in the only place he couldn't follow her to.

In the ladies' room, Desiree went into a stall and sat down on the closed toilet seat. Decker had dated that snake in stilettos? How could he fall in love with Yolanda Reynolds and be attracted to *her*? It made no sense. She and Yolanda were nothing alike. But then, some men didn't care about a woman's character as long as she was sexy and beautiful, and Yolanda had those attributes in spades. She just didn't have a heart.

"This is ridiculous," she said softly as she rose. "I'm not staying in the bathroom because my date used to date my high school bully."

"Did you say something?" the woman in the next stall asked. "Are you out of toilet paper? I've got plenty over here."

"No, thank you," Desiree said, and walked out of the stall. She went to a sink and splashed water on her face. Dabbing it dry, she smiled at herself. For a moment the same insecure feeling she used to get when Yolanda and her clique of mean girls would corner her at her locker and harass her mercilessly had come over her. On one hand, Yolanda and her friends had made going to school back then pure hell, but on the other, if not for that experience, she probably wouldn't be a psychologist today. It was the bullying that had inspired an interest in finding out why people behaved the way they did.

She fixed her makeup, smiled at herself again and left the bathroom. Decker had been forthcoming with her, revealing the identity of the woman who had broken his heart. The least she could do was be equally forthcoming with him. Let the cards fall where they might.

When she got back to the table, Decker eyed her with concern as he rose and pulled out her chair for her once more. She smiled up at him. "Thank you."

He sat down across from her. "Are you all right?"

Desiree took a swallow of her wine. Setting the

glass on the table, she met his eyes. "I don't suppose Yolanda told you what her high school days were like?"

He looked puzzled, which didn't surprise her. He'd seemed pretty shocked by her behavior when she abruptly left for the bathroom in order to compose herself.

"Only a few things, like she was homecoming queen, head cheerleader and was in the drama club."

Desiree forced a smile. Yolanda *would* tell him only the positive things she'd done in high school. Who would brag about being a bully? That was a bit too much truth when you were trying to impress a man.

She tried a different approach. "Were you ever picked on when you were a kid?"

Decker laughed shortly. "I was big for my age, and studying kung fu. Nobody messed with me."

Desiree realized trying to find common ground with Decker wasn't going to work. He continued to look at her with concern written all over his face. Perhaps he was regretting all those months of asking her out only to learn that she was not the woman he thought she would be. The mental health professional possibly suffered from a mental illness herself.

"You're lucky," Desiree said, looking him straight in the eye. "From ninth grade to twelfth, your ex-girlfriend made it her business to make sure I knew she and her friends couldn't stand me. She would leave disgusting notes on my locker. Her nickname for me was Nappyrella, a combination of the words *nappy* and Cinderella, because I wore my hair natural and they didn't approve of that style. Once they enlisted the help of a guy they knew I had a crush on to pull a practical joke on me. He asked me to a school dance and on the night of the dance, he didn't show up. The next day they'd plastered photos of him and another girl at the dance, having a great time together, on my locker. They had a lot of fun at my expense."

Decker went to her, knelt beside her chair and pulled her into his arms. "I knew she was evil, just not *how* evil. Damn, Desi, why didn't you kick her ass?" He leaned away in order to meet her gaze. Desiree fought back tears. She was touched by his gesture.

"You know why," she said, smiling.

"Because we're taught not to use our skills against anyone except to protect our lives or the lives of others," he said, quoting one of the credos martial artists lived by.

"Exactly," Desiree said. She gently touched his cheek. "Now go back to your seat. People are staring."

He hugged her tighter. "I don't care if they stare." But he let go of her and returned to his seat nonetheless.

They sat for a moment simply smiling at each other. Then they picked up their forks and continued eating the delicious meals in front of them.

Desiree broke the silence five minutes later with "You dodged a bullet when she broke up with you."

"I know," Decker said, and laughed softly. "Thanks for sharing your story with me. It makes me even more grateful that she chose Hollywood over me."

After dinner they went to a bar on Glenwood Avenue that had live blues and jazz on weekends. The crowd was multicultural, and the décor like a Chicago speakeasy in the twenties or thirties. A blues band commanded the red-velvet-draped stage tonight. When Decker and Desiree entered, the male singer was doing a good rendition of Otis Redding's "Try a Little Tenderness."

Decker pulled out Desiree's chair for her, and they sat down to enjoy the performance. The lighting was dim, and candles in squat red glass jars rested in the center of the tables. A waitress made a beeline for them as soon as they sat down. "Would you like something to drink?" Decker asked, deferring to Desiree. Desiree was looking around the room, enjoying the laid-back atmosphere. "What kind of nonalcoholic drinks do you have?"

The waitress, a young African-American woman with a short Afro, smiled and said, "The bartender can make you a virgin daiquiri, or just about any other drink. We also have bottled water, regular and sparkling, juices and soft drinks."

"Just bring me a sparkling water with a twist of lime, please," Desiree said.

The waitress turned to look at Decker, her smile growing wider. "And what can I bring you, sir?"

"I'll take water, too," he said.

In the waitress's absence, he said, "I'm driving, and the wine with dinner was enough for one night."

The singer had begun Stevie Wonder's "Higher Ground." Couples danced to the upbeat tune. Decker stood and reached for Desiree's hand. She didn't hesitate, and soon they were one of many couples moving around the dance floor with a syncopated beat.

Decker liked the way Desiree moved. Obviously, she loved to dance. It was evident in the sway of her hips, the natural rhythm she displayed and the look of joy in her eyes that held his gaze so compellingly. They did a sort of hip-hop version of a swing dance, moving effortlessly together as though this were not the first time they'd done this. Her fit yet voluptuous body, with curves in all the right places, was hard to tear his eyes from, but he kept his gaze on hers. It was more intimate. He hoped he was reading her right, because those dark brown–rimmed golden eyes were telling him she was digging him. Not only enjoying being with him, but interested in the prospect of seeing more of him. He hoped so because he'd definitely loved being with her tonight.

He still couldn't quite wrap his mind around the fact that his ex had bullied her in high school. What were the odds that he'd wind up meeting, and dating, the woman his ex had tormented so many years ago? It almost felt like fate to him, and he generally didn't believe in fate or coincidences, and definitely not fairy tales. In his experience, life held no magic, just your daily grind. Desiree almost made him believe.

The band slowed it down with "A Sunday Kind of Love" by Etta James. Decker pulled Desiree into his arms. Now, this was what he'd been waiting for. Their cheeks touched briefly, and then her head was on his shoulder and she relaxed in his embrace. He breathed her in and relaxed himself. She smelled like fresh flowers. The warmth of her body permeated his clothing, penetrating his skin, making him instantly on guard for a hard-on. The last thing he needed was for Desiree to pull back from him after feeling his erection on her thigh. Not good. Not on the first date. The things a man had to worry about!

She suddenly raised her head and looked into his eyes, smiling. "Your mother taught you well," she said, her tone husky.

He tightened the embrace a smidgen. "Mama never prepared me for a woman like you."

She looked intrigued. Her eyes held an amused glint in them. "And what kind of woman am I?"

"Don't be coy, Desi. You know you're sexy as hell."

"I know I have an unsettling effect on some men, but it's been a long time since I used my sexual mojo on anyone. I'm a bit rusty."

She hadn't denied she was sexy. That made him respect her more. He liked that she accepted who she was and didn't try to pretend to be something she wasn't.

"You have my permission to practice on me," he said with a confident smile.

That was when she tiptoed and kissed him on

the mouth. He had to admit, the move took him by surprise, but only for a second or two. Then it was on. For the longest time, he'd been wondering what it would feel like to kiss her. Now he knew. It was bliss itself. Her lips were full, juicy and sweeter than anything he'd ever experienced before. Her breath mingled with his and created an airborne aphrodisiac. Honestly, she tasted like heaven, a feast for a love-starved man who'd just been invited to an all-you-can-eat buffet. He had to force himself to hold back, because damn, the woman had made him wait forever for this kiss. Just as he got control of his enthusiasm, she slipped her tongue in his mouth, and the sensual nature of the act caused him to slip further under her spell. They were still kissing when the song ended. Some part of his feverish brain imparted that bit of information to him. But it wasn't until the couples around them started whooping and hollering encouragement to them that they came to their senses and parted.

He ushered an embarrassed-looking Desiree back to their table. She laughed quietly. "I guess I'm hungrier for human contact than I thought."

Decker leaned toward her across the tiny round table and took her hand in his. He sought her gaze, but she shyly lowered her head. "Desiree, look at me."

She raised her head and looked him in the eye. He smiled. "Feel free to lavish all your affection on me. I'm big and strong, I can take it, and if it kills me, so be it. I'd die happy."

She burst out laughing. "Why did it take me so long to say yes to you?"

"We're together now, and that's all that matters." He squeezed her hand affectionately.

Desiree was looking deeply into Decker's eyes after returning from the dance floor when she heard another woman calling his name excitedly.

She raised her head and saw a tall, shapely woman in a very short black leather skirt, low-cut sleeveless red silk pullover top and black stilettos. Her black hair fell in waves down her back, and her full lips were bloodred. "Decker Riley," she cooed as she stood next to their table. No, Desiree corrected herself, she wasn't standing; she was leaning over the table, her ample chest nearly in Decker's face.

Decker sat back as far away from the woman as he could get, and Desiree saw he was having a hard time controlling his irritation at this intrusion. His eyes narrowed as he regarded the woman. "Hello, Marisa."

He turned to Desiree. "Desiree, this is Marisa Carlton. She used to work for the firm."

"Hello, Marisa," Desiree said, keeping her tone friendly.

Marisa looked at her, dismissively rolled her eyes, and then sidled closer to Decker. "I always said that if I ever saw you out in public I would give you a piece of my mind for firing me. But I'm too much of a lady to do that." She reached into her purse and withdrew a card. "Now that fraternization is off the table, call me. I'll make you regret letting me go."

Desiree was not even shocked by the woman's behavior. In her practice she'd heard, and seen, much worse. She was pleasantly surprised by Decker's reaction, though. He nailed Marisa with a hard stare. Marisa seemed hypnotized by his gaze and couldn't tear her eyes from his. Not raising his voice, he said, as he placed the card firmly back in her palm, "You've been exceedingly disrespectful to my date and to me, Marisa. So I don't regret saying that firing you was not only the right thing to do, but the only thing to do. You have no regard for boundaries. You were often late, didn't perform your job well and blatantly flaunted your sexuality in a professional environment where it was highly inappropriate to do so. Now, please leave before I have you thrown out."

For a moment Desiree thought Marisa was going to put up a fight. She puffed up her chest, and a determined light entered her dark eyes, but only seconds later, she let out a defeated sigh, muttered, "To hell with you," and turned and walked away.

Decker shook his head in consternation. "I fired her because she kept coming on to me even after I repeatedly told her I wasn't interested."

To Desiree, this was a perfect example of why she'd resisted going out with Decker for so long. Women threw themselves at him. Was that what had happened with Noel? Maybe he'd tried to remain faithful to her, but temptation had been too irresistible. Was there any man on earth who could remain faithful to one woman?

But was it fair to Decker to judge him by Noel's standards? He had, after all, refused to sleep with Marisa when she'd offered herself to him.

Decker was looking at her askance. "Desi, what are you thinking?"

"I bet women try to proposition you all the time," she said.

"Women are bolder than they used to be," Decker allowed. He reached across the table and grasped her hands in his. "You don't have to worry about that. I'm a one-woman man. I'm faithful when I'm in a committed relationship, Desi. That's just how I'm wired. Like your promise to yourself to only sleep with someone you're in love with. When I'm in love with a woman, I don't sleep with anyone else."

"Why'd you have to turn out so damned fine?" Desiree exclaimed in exasperation.

Decker laughed. "Are you going to hold an accident of birth against me? It's not my fault that my parents' genes gave me this face. Besides, *you're* beautiful. Am I supposed to distrust you just because other men find you attractive? That's not reasonable, Desi. In every relationship you've got to have a certain amount of faith that the one you love will stay true to you. Otherwise it won't work."

"After finding out about Noel's cheating, it's going to take me a while to believe in fidelity again, especially when you look like that!" She accusingly pointed at his handsome face and physique.

Decker just laughed harder. "Girl, I've got to give it to you, being with you is never boring. Are you ready to go home?"

Desiree smiled and nodded. She rose and picked up her purse. "Some first date, huh?"

"It was going pretty well up until a few minutes ago," Decker said as they made their way across the club to the exit.

Chapter 6

Desiree heard her cell phone ringing on the nightstand, but she was so deep in a delicious dream about Decker that she was reluctant to come fully awake. Her dream self kept saying, *Let me dream, let me dream.* However, the ringing was too insistent, and the cacophony finally broke through the barrier of the dream. She groaned as she opened her eyes and rolled over in bed to pick up the phone and check the display. She knew it! It was one of her sisters. Saturday morning, and (she checked the current time on the cell phone) she was half an hour late for their jog in the park.

Lauren's voice said, "Last week when Colton and I stayed up late, at least I made it to the park on time the next morning."

"I'm sorry, but you know I'm not used to late hours," Desiree said as she hauled herself up and put her feet on the floor. That was a start, although what she really wanted to do was go back to bed.

"What time did you get in last night?"

"Two-thirty," she said, yawning. "We had dinner and went dancing. Then Decker brought me home and I invited him in for a coffee, which, thank God, he declined, because if he had accepted he might still be here."

Lauren was laughing on the other end. Desiree heard her trying to relay the message to Meghan between guffaws.

"I'm getting up now," she said into the phone. She yawned again.

"Will you stop yawning in my ear?" Lauren said. "Go back to bed. Missing one Saturday won't kill you. We'll talk later. I just wanted to call you and tell you, I told you so! It's hard to resist a Riley man."

Meghan got on the line. "Don't forget we're getting together on Sunday at Lauren's to discuss Mama and Daddy's anniversary party. I had a conversation over Skype with Petra early this morning, she contacts me at the most godforsaken hours because of the time change, but I'm rambling. Long story short, she's coming home. Her research is done in Central Africa for the time being. She said a TV network is interested in her hosting a show for them. Could be *Animal Planet*, I can't recall. But she's thinking of taking the job and staying stateside for a while."

Desiree was fully awake now. "That's great news. It'll be wonderful having P back in the fold."

"You're telling me!" Meghan exclaimed. "I can't wait. Okay, sis, get some rest. Are you seeing Decker again tonight?"

"Yes, this time he's cooking for me at his place. He'll be grilling for me."

"Men and their grills," Meghan joked. "They've loved grilling since the first caveman discovered fire."

Desiree heard her tell Lauren what she'd said about Decker cooking for her at his place tonight, shortly after which Lauren took the phone from Meghan and said, "No, Desi, do not, I repeat, *do not* go to Decker's place tonight or any night soon. You're not ready to sleep with him."

"Who said anything about sleeping with him?" Desiree asked, her voice rising. She certainly had no intention of sleeping with Decker after the Marisa incident. Not until she felt more secure in the notion that faithfulness was possible between them. But she was determined to give their relationship a fighting chance.

"I haven't heard you say anything about *not* sleeping with him, either," Lauren countered. "It's going to be hard to resist him after he's cooked for you. Riley men wield spatulas like magic wands. They cook for you, pour on the charm, and before you know it you're lying naked in their arms."

"May I remind you that you slept with Colton the

first night you met him?" Desiree said. "And you two ended up married with an adorable son."

"Colton and I made love for all the wrong reasons," Lauren said regrettably. "I was hurting over a bad marriage that ended in divorce, and he was seeking comfort because his dad had just died. That we ended up falling in love was a miracle. Many couples who make love too soon don't end up together." She paused. "Who am I talking to? You know the statistics, Dr. Gaines. How many divorced people come to you for help? Quite a few, I'd wager."

"Too many," Desiree admitted. "But you don't have to worry, sis. I'll sleep with Decker only if I fall in love with him."

"Are you sure you're not already in love with him?" asked Lauren. "It's not as if you just met him. He's been a part of your life for a while now. He was on the periphery of your life, yes, but you two ran into each other at countless family gatherings. Maybe subconsciously you not only lusted after him, but learned to love him for who he is. Admit it, you've liked him all along. You were just afraid of letting Noel's memory go. But now that you know Noel was no knight in shining armor, psychologically you're free to love again."

"Who's the psychologist here?" Desiree asked with a laugh.

Lauren laughed, too. "I just know you. I'm the older sister. Heed my advice. Don't go to Decker's place tonight. Go to a movie or something."

"I'll give it some thought," Desiree finally promised Lauren. "Goodbye, sis. I'm going back to bed."

"Bye, girl," Lauren said, and hung up.

Desiree hung up the phone and lay back down. As she adjusted her pillow, getting comfortable, thoughts of the kisses she'd shared with Decker flashed through her mind. Was she simply horny, or were those the best kisses she'd ever had? She smiled as she closed her eyes and willed herself to go back into that wonderful dream she'd been having about Decker before Lauren had interrupted her. "Dream, dream," she whispered as she drifted off to sleep.

Desiree was in her bedroom getting dressed for her date with Decker, the TV on the wall tuned to the evening news, when she heard the anchor talking about a teacher who'd been arrested for allegedly having a sexual relationship with one of his students.

She went to stand in front of the screen, her eyes riveted on footage of the suspect as he was led from his home, handcuffed, to a waiting police cruiser. It could be none other than Madison's math teacher, Fredric Sawyer. He was a bespectacled, mild-mannered-looking guy who appeared to be in his midthirties. On Wednesday, after she'd had a breakthrough with Madison, Mrs. Samuelson had taken her daughter home, saying they would be going to the police station to file charges against Sawyer as soon as Madison felt strong enough to face all the questioning that would undoubtedly ensue.

On the screen, Sawyer was holding his head down

as though he didn't want his face to be seen. A reporter was thrusting a microphone under his nose, asking, "Did you take advantage of a fifteen-year-old girl? Would you like the opportunity to deny the charges?"

Sawyer refused to say anything and looked relieved when the officer helped him into the cruiser, making sure he didn't hit his head while getting in. The reporter turned to the camera at this point and said, "Sawyer isn't saying much of anything. Janie, I'm told that Sawyer is married with two small children. We tried to speak with his wife, but she wouldn't open the door and talk to us."

"Leave the poor woman alone," Desiree mumbled as she watched. The news then cut to an anchor in the studio who must have been the Janie the reporter had referred to. Blond and beautifully made up, she smiled and said, "We'll have more later on this breaking story."

Desiree wondered how Madison was faring. Surely she was aware that Sawyer had been arrested. She had given Madison her cell number and made her promise to call her anytime, day or night, if she needed her. She hoped the girl would keep her promise and not suffer quietly if this new development caused her any emotional distress. Desiree felt compelled to get in her car and drive to the Samuelson house just in case Madison needed her, but that wouldn't be advisable. She had to allow Madison to start making decisions for herself. She'd been a pawn in Sawyer's sick game for so long. She now had to reclaim control of herself, her inner strength and ultimately her own power.

There was no harm in phoning Mrs. Samuelson and checking up on Madison, though. She picked up her cell phone from the nightstand and scrolled down to the programmed number. The phone rang only twice before Serena Samuelson answered, "Dr. Gaines, you've heard, huh?"

"Yes," Desiree answered. "I'm just calling to let you know that I'm at your disposal if you need me." Her voice was soft yet reassuring. "How is Madison doing? Did she watch the news?"

"Yes, we all saw it," Serena said. "Madison isn't saying much, but I think it's safe to say that she got some satisfaction out of seeing him being led away by the police."

"As well she should," Desiree said. "All right, I'll let you get back to her. Give her my best and remind her that she's not alone. She has many people around her who love her."

"I will, Doctor, and thank you," said Serena.

Desiree ended the call feeling a little more settled. She knew this was only the beginning. Anything could happen before Sawyer saw the inside of a prison.

Decker pulled up in front of Desiree's house and cut the engine. He sat for a moment, looking at the house, a large Mediterranean-style home on a quiet, tree-lined street. The landscaping was very well done. He couldn't imagine Desiree got out there in the heat of the day and cut the grass herself, but he wouldn't put it past her. She seemed to enjoy using her body in physical ways. Between the karate and the running, she seemed to be in perpetual motion. He liked that because he was quite active himself. A woman who could keep up with him and perhaps join him in his interests intrigued him.

He got out of the SUV wearing jeans, a baby-blue T-shirt with the emblem of his alma mater, the University of North Carolina, emblazoned on his chest, and athletic shoes. He'd told Desiree he would pick her up at seven. When he told her he would pick her up, she'd protested, saying she would drive. But he'd insisted that picking her up and bringing her safely back home again was the gentlemanly thing to do. She'd seemed a little surprised by his attitude, but pleased, too.

He jogged the rest of the way up the walk and rang the bell. He looked around him as he waited. Desiree had a way of making a home very welcoming. Even the plants surrounding the portico seemed to give evidence of a loving nature. He recognized blooming orchids in pots, hanging ferns and climbing roses encircling the columns holding up the portico. It was a very serene setting.

But the barefoot woman who opened the door made that sedate feeling vanish and forced him to replace it with one of intense longing as soon as he laid eyes on her. Desiree was dressed in a short hot-pink dress that hugged her curves. The stretchy material twisted around her graceful neck, which sent the eye directly to her full breasts. He allowed his gaze to continue downward over her hourglass figure with its flat stomach and flaring hips, ending at her long, shapely legs.

She grinned at him. "Hey, come on in. You want a tour before we go? We didn't spend much time in the house last night."

She stepped backward to allow him to enter. Decker didn't know if it was okay to kiss her hello or not. He wished he could shake this insecurity about Desiree, but he didn't want to make any missteps now that they were actually dating. He waited for some sign from her. She didn't make him wait long. She hugged him enthusiastically. Enveloped in the lovely scent of her, this time a spicy oriental fragrance, he closed his eyes as she squeezed him tightly, and hugged her back.

Parting, they looked into each other's eyes and then she said, "Kiss me already!"

Decker leaned down, placed his big right hand behind her head, grasped her about the waist with his left and pulled her against him, claiming her mouth.

He claimed it and planted his flag on it in his own inimitable fashion. He could not kiss Desiree in a heated rush. He approached her with appreciation for the sweetness that she offered up to him. Yes, he was excited, but it was not an out-of-control excitement that would render the experience nothing more than a sexual response when he thought about the encounter later on. He intended to relish the here and now. He savored the fact that her lips were soft and that her breath tasted sweet and fresh and was beguilingly intoxicating. His ears were attuned to the soft mewling noise she made as she kissed him, which told him she was enjoying this as much as he was. He exulted in the fact that her arms had naturally gone around his neck, and she was pulling him closer to her. She wanted her body molded to his.

When he raised his head, she looked at him with a satisfied smile. "I could get used to you in a hot minute, Decker Riley."

She took his hand and led him farther inside, pausing to close the front door. Turning back around, she said, "Welcome to my African-Greek-inspired oasis."

As he walked down the couple of steps that led from the front door into the foyer, he looked up at the high ceiling. Hanging from the ceiling was a chandelier with crystals that produced a golden light. "African-Greek-inspired?" he said, curious as to why she'd described the house that way.

As they walked past the foyer into the great room, Desiree said, "The Greeks built their homes in an open style so that the air flow would keep them cool in summer. The Africans, who also had to build with hot weather in mind, built houses that would allow them to breathe in hot, humid climates. I love the open concept, so when you walk in you have a line of sight straight through the kitchen, the great room and to the back door. Most days I don't have to run the air conditioner. I can just open my front and back doors and the air circulates throughout the entire house, cooling it."

Decker was impressed. He'd simply chosen

his loft because it was big and modern, giving no thought whatsoever to the environment. Desiree was already being a good influence on him.

The whole house had either tile or hardwood floors. She took him upstairs and showed him her bedroom. He had to admit that he got a little turned on after seeing the size of her bed. It was large enough to accommodate him. This, he knew, was wishful thinking. He didn't expect to be invited to her bed anytime soon. "I live in a loft," he said. "For some reason I think of houses as places where families live."

Desiree was showing him the guest room, a large room down the hall from her bedroom, which had its own bath. "I used to think that way, too," she said. "But I woke one morning, still single at twenty-nine, and said to myself, What am I waiting for? I earn my own money. I'm perfectly capable of buying a house, an investment, instead of paying rent every month. So I went out the next week and started looking at houses."

"Oh, I own my loft," Decker was quick to say. "It's more of a bachelor pad than it is a home, though. You'll understand when you see it later." He gestured around them. "I don't have your homey touch. This house feels welcoming."

The furnishings were a mixture of contemporary with a smattering of antiques. The combination lent an air of sophistication and comfort at the same time.

"I'm sure your space feels welcoming to your guests," Desiree said.

"You'll see soon enough," Decker said. "Are you ready to go?"

Desiree let go of his hand and hurried back down the hallway to her bedroom. "Just let me put on some shoes and grab my purse."

Decker was right, Desiree decided after spending five minutes in his loft. This was a spaceship. The loft had plenty of room and was ultramodern. The kitchen was a chef's dream, with all the bells and whistles: the latest stainless-steel gas range, fridge, dishwasher, soft-close drawers. The colors were monochromatic. Desiree wondered what Decker had against a little color. The place was very clean, almost sterile. But it lacked warmth. On the other hand, it was the perfect man cave. And it probably fit his needs just so. Wasn't a home supposed to be designed to suit those who lived in it? And it was obvious his home was designed specifically for him. Because he liked to cook, the kitchen was outfitted for ease of movement in that space. A large balcony, complete with a top-of-the-line gas grill and comfortable patio furniture, was the ideal place where a man could prepare his favorite meal of steak and potatoes. And the living room was tricked out with the latest electronics—a big-screen TV on the wall and an expensive stereo system replete with wireless speakers. Any man would love to live here.

"Feel free to have a look around," Decker had said a few minutes ago when they got here. "I'm going to put the steaks on the grill."

"Want some help?" she'd asked, hoping he'd say no so she could look around on her own. She couldn't help it. She was a snoop, albeit a harmless one. She'd never stoop to going through his medicine cabinet, for example. She just wanted to see how he lived without his being there watching her reaction.

So now she was walking through his house while he was in the kitchen preparing the steaks for the grill. She strolled into the living room and went to check out the CDs on the shelf near the stereo. She smiled when she saw what a neat freak he was. The loft itself was very clean, thanks to a cleaning service, no doubt.

However, that wasn't the only thing that told her he was a bit of an obsessive when it came to order. His CDs were alphabetized, whereas her CDs were shelved in no particular order. Sometimes it took her several minutes to locate a favorite CD. With Decker's, all she had to do was think of an artist's name, then look in the section that began with the first letter of his/her last name. Curious about his taste in the blues, she went to the K section. Sure enough, he had several B. B. King CDs. She doubted he owned any of Koko Taylor's albums, so she went to the *T*'s. He had one Koko Taylor CD, but it was a collection of her greatest hits. Desiree put it in the player, and the rough, soulful voice of the late, great blues singer began belting out "Born Under a Bad Sign."

She closed her eyes and swayed to the music, feeling the sensuality of the beat infuse her body.

She started when she heard Decker say from behind her, "I like that. Who is it?"

She turned to face him. He was wearing an apron with Kiss the Cook on it, along with the image of a pair of juicy red lips.

"I'm not surprised you don't know who it is," she said as she walked into his open arms. "You only have one of her CDs. Have you ever listened to it?"

His gray eyes squinted in concentration. "Mmm, let me see, is it Etta James?"

Desiree gave him a disgusted look. "Not even!"

"Sarah Vaughn?"

"Your blues education is sorely lacking. Sarah Vaughn was a jazz singer, one of the best!"

"Then I did get Etta James's genre right? She sang the blues?"

"Yes, she was a blues singer. She and the woman singing now are my two favorite female blues singers who have passed on. My favorite living female blues singer is Shemekia Copeland."

"I've got it, then," Decker said, triumphant. "It's Koko Taylor."

Desiree looked suspicious. "How did you get that?"

"Last night," he explained, "when you listed your favorite singers, you only mentioned two women—Etta James and Koko Taylor."

"And you remembered what I said?" She was genuinely impressed.

"I remember everything you say to me," Decker said as he bent low to gently kiss her cheek. "I remember the day we met as though it were yesterday.

I remember how thrilled I was to find you at my aunt Veronica's a few hours later, eating collard greens with her in her kitchen after Uncle Frank's funeral."

Desiree's heart raced. She felt tears welling up at the sincere tone of his voice, and the sheer honesty that shone in his eyes. She was also remembering what Veronica had told her about him that day in her kitchen—that he was a good guy and that the player act was just a facade to hide his insecurities.

She now wished she had let down her guard with him then. But there was no going back. There was only today and tomorrow. For today, she was going to make up for lost time and kiss the hell out of him.

"I was so cold to you that day," she murmured regrettably.

"You didn't know me," he said softly, his eyes boring into hers. "Of course you would be wary of a strange guy who kept staring at you as if he'd never seen anything so beautiful. I made a fool of myself."

"I'm sorry you feel that way," she said softly as she stood on tiptoe. "Because, looking back, I think you were very sweet."

She kissed him. His arms went around her, and she felt herself being lifted off the floor in power-ful arms. Suddenly she was weightless and flying. He was gentle yet intense, the kiss deep and soul-stirring. Her body went weak. Desire, like a drug, shot through her, melting her resistance and making her nerve endings sing and moistness gather between her legs. Her nipples hardened, and when Decker let go of her and took a step back, as though he knew they were dangerously close to going too far, she knew evidence of her arousal was visible through the silken material of her bra.

His eyes raked over her body before he visibly gained control by taking a deep breath. "I'd better go check on the steaks. Don't want them to burn."

"Put me to work," Desiree said, following him. "I need to stay busy."

"You can make the salad," he said over his shoulder as he led the way to the kitchen.

In the kitchen, she went to the fridge to get the salad ingredients from the crisper. Taking everything over to the sink, she watched him a moment as he turned the steaks on the grill on the gas range.

She began washing the lettuce. "I'm having a hard time resisting you."

He looked at her with those expressive gray eyes and smiled. "Imagine how I feel. I've been half in love with you for months. Multiply your efforts to resist me by about a hundred."

Hearing him say that just made her want him more. She sighed and lowered her eyes to her task. "It would be a mistake to go to bed this early in our relationship."

"I know," he said. "That doesn't stop me from wanting to."

"Me, either," she assured him.

"That music doesn't help," he said. Koko Taylor was singing "I'm a Woman." It was a declaration of the power a woman wields simply because she is born a woman. Desiree had always loved that song. Listening to it made her feel powerful and extremely sexy.

"I'll go change it," she said, dropping the lettuce into the sink and grabbing a paper towel from the holder on the counter.

"Don't bother," Decker said. "Doing that won't help. I'm still going to want you." He smiled at her. "Let's face it, Desi, nothing's going to extinguish this feeling except making love to you. And the way I feel about you, even that won't help for long because afterward I'm going to want to make love to you again and again."

He set down the fork with which he'd turned the steaks and faced her. "But I'm not a kid who can't control his impulses. I'll wait for you as long as it takes."

Desiree's body fairly thrummed with pent-up sexual tension. However, she knew he was right. It was too early to go to bed with him. She forced a smile. "It's a deal," she said, then tossed the crumpled-up paper towel into the nearby wastebasket.

"Excuse me." She walked swiftly from the room, heading to the bathroom. She needed to splash water on her face and pull herself together.

Chapter 7

Two weeks after Frederic Sawyer's arrest, Madison told Desiree that somehow it had gotten out that it was she who had accused him of molesting her. She'd been cornered at her locker at school by several girls who made it clear that they didn't believe her and were supporting Sawyer. They called her a troublemaker and told her she was ruining his career and tearing his family apart with her lies.

Desiree had been so angered by this that she had gone to the police station and spoken with the lead detective on the case. He assured her that no one in the department had leaked Madison's identity to either the press or any private citizen. He suggested that Sawyer had told someone close to him, and that person had spread the rumor.

Desiree knew that was a possibility, but that didn't help Madison. Desiree wanted to advise her to stay home from school, but she didn't because that would be defeating the purpose of getting her to believe in herself and stop allowing anyone to exert control over her. At any rate, Madison didn't seem unduly upset by the development. She'd looked Desiree in the eye and said, "I don't care what anyone says or does. They won't chase me away from school. I have a right to be there. I haven't done anything wrong. I'm trying to make sure he doesn't hurt anyone else."

It was one of the proudest days of Desiree's career. Madison was growing into a strong young woman with a healthy sense of right and wrong. Frederic Sawyer, however, appeared to be a beaten man. News reports said his wife, needing to protect her children from the bad publicity, had gone on an extended visit to her parents in another state. Sawyer was so despondent he refused to speak with the public defender assigned to his case. He seemed not to care what happened to him.

Desiree was also kept busy planning her parents' thirty-fifth wedding anniversary surprise party with her sisters. It was set for the end of July, and they were going to pull out all the stops. The biggest surprise would be Petra's return from Africa. Her parents had no idea she was coming home.

One Saturday night in early July, about four months after she and Decker had gone on their first date, Desiree invited him over for dinner.

She set the table on the patio and put on her new

pale pink sleeveless sundress that cinched her waist, with a hem that fell a couple of inches above her knees. She felt like a fifties bombshell in it. To further the effect, she styled her hair in an upswept do, and put on matching pink three-inch pumps. Hot-pink lipstick made her lips look bee-stung and highly kissable.

When the bell rang, she paused to look at herself one last time in the mirror over the foyer table before opening the door.

There was an apprehensive expression in her eyes. She knew it was because she planned to tell Decker she loved him tonight. The past one hundred and twenty days of close proximity with him, revealing their souls to each other and simply watching him interact with friends and family, as she'd been doing for more than two years now, all had served to solidify her feelings for him. He was a good man. She believed her heart was safe in his hands. Now she was going to trust him with the rest of her.

She opened the door and Decker, dressed in jeans, a short-sleeve denim shirt and black athletic shoes, grinned widely and pulled her into his arms.

Desiree experienced that excited yet secure sensation she always got when his muscular arms went around her. She inhaled the clean, freshly showered scent of him.

He lowered his head, his gray eyes looking deeply into hers. "Damn, you feel good. I couldn't get through the day fast enough, knowing I was seeing you tonight." Then he kissed her.

Although the word *kiss*, Desiree thought as his mouth claimed hers, was not descriptive enough to fully explain the metamorphosis that occurred in her body when his mouth covered hers. First, there was the anticipation of the pleasure to come. It made her start tingling all over. Then his firm, yet soft lips touched hers, and nerve endings started to sing. While the choir belted out a rousing Hallelujah, his tongue begged for entrance to her inner sanctum, which she eagerly granted. Once that was achieved, she was lost and floated on a cloud of happiness whose duration she wanted to extend to infinity.

All too soon, though, the kiss was broken off, and it always left her feeling a little sad and wanting more.

This time when they parted, she sighed contentedly, smiled and said, "I'm literally high on you."

Decker's smile was cocky. "I aim to please!"

She laughed and playfully punched him on the arm. "Don't let that ego get too big. Come on, I made my mother's oven-fried chicken."

"Mmm," Decker said as he followed her to the kitchen. "I love your mother's chicken. How is the party planning coming along, by the way? Miss Virginia isn't getting suspicious as their anniversary date gets closer, is she?"

Desiree looked back at him over her shoulder. She knew he was checking her out. He had a habit of hanging back and watching. And she loved it. It had been so long since a man showed an appreciation of her womanly charms. At least a man she wanted to notice. There were always men who flirted and tried to get her in bed without investing any time and effort. She took pleasure in letting them know in no uncertain terms that it was never going to happen.

"Nothing gets pulled over Virginia Gaines's eyes," she said of her mother's uncanny ability to avoid being surprised. "She already knows there's going to be a party. What she doesn't know is that Petra will be there. This year we'll get her!"

In the kitchen, Desiree removed the pan of chicken from the oven and began putting some on a plate. "I set the table on the patio," she said.

Decker, who wasn't the sort of man to allow his woman to wait on him hand and foot, was getting the bowl of salad from the fridge while they talked. "Sounds good," he said. "But I have to warn you, the sky looked a little dark when I was driving over."

"Let's take a chance," Desiree said as she grabbed the salad dressing and headed out the French doors. She had already put crusty French bread and tall glasses with ice in them on the table. "Oh, would you grab the pitcher of iced tea in the fridge before you come out?" she said as an afterthought. "Or I have some chilled white wine if you prefer."

"No, iced tea is good," Decker said, turning to get the iced tea.

Soon they were seated at the round, umbrella-topped table. The scent of night-blooming jasmine was carried on the evening breezes, and the surrounding garden, boasting a host of spring flowers and abundant greenery, lent a calming effect to the setting.

"So, tell me how your week was," Desiree said before biting into a chicken leg.

"Chaotic, as usual," Decker replied. "But I'd think something was wrong if it wasn't. I prefer to be too busy than not busy enough."

"Any interesting new cases?" she asked.

"I'm representing a teen accused of killing his girlfriend," Decker said.

"How do you decide to take a case like that?"

"It depends," he said. He paused to finish chewing a mouthful of salad. "I believe everyone has the right to a fair trial, so I try not to be judgmental. But when murder is involved, the case has to satisfy two criteria for me—do I believe the defendant is innocent? Or do I believe he's guilty, but he did it in a fit of passion or madness? If so, I'll defend him to the best of my abilities."

"That seems fair," Desiree said.

"Don't get me wrong," Decker said, looking her in the eye. "I'm no saint. When I started out, I would defend anyone who could pay me the big bucks. But as time passed, I was no longer able to stomach the real scumbags. They were coming to me in droves because of my reputation in the courtroom. My soul, though, was suffering because of it. These days, I choose whom I defend more carefully."

Desiree reached across the table and affectionately squeezed his hand. "I love that about you."

Decker smiled at her and squeezed her hand back. "Enough about me," he said. "How is that girl doing who turned her teacher in and is now being harassed at school?"

Desiree was pleased he was concerned about Madison. She, of course, had not told him anything personal about Madison's case, like her name or the name of her molester. That was privileged information. "She's getting stronger every day," she said. "I've often seen that happen when a girl actively starts taking back her power."

"I'm glad," Decker said. "I hate it when children are preyed on. It's tough enough growing up without having to deal with that."

Desiree sighed inwardly. No wonder she loved this man. She hoped he wanted children, because she wanted a houseful. With that thought, she blushed.

Decker must have seen the change in her facial expression, because he laughed shortly and said, "What?"

She looked straight into his eyes as if she could distract him by showing him she had nothing to hide. "What do you mean?"

"Desiree, I've been watching you for months now. I'm your ex-stalker, remember? I've watched you from across a crowded room. I've watched you laughing and talking with your crazy sisters. I love them all, but they're crazy. I've watched you gossiping with my aunt Veronica. I've watched you eating chocolate cake, which, for some weird reason, turns me on. I know when you're embarrassed, and something you were thinking a minute ago embarrassed you. What was it?"

"Damned lawyers," Desiree grumbled.

To which Decker laughed heartily. "Go ahead, insult the lawyer. We're used to it. That doesn't mean I'm going away. What were you thinking?"

Suddenly thunder rumbled, and rain began falling in sheets. They quickly gathered plates, glasses and cutlery and raced inside, laughing all the way. "So much for dining al fresco," Desiree said. They piled all the dishes in the sink for later, and eyed each other in all their drenched glory. Desiree's hair lay limp down her back. Her dress was plastered to her body. She looked at Decker. His clothing clung to his body, outlining his sexy, muscular form. She had yet to see him naked because she had not given him the green light.

Love came hard for her. In spite of her resolve to be open to love, it eluded her. She didn't trust her ability to discern true love when she saw it. She had loved Noel, or thought so. Admittedly she had never felt this much desire for Noel. But these feelings could be because she hadn't been with a man in years. She hadn't wanted to make love to Decker until she was certain she loved him. Anything less would be unfair to him. He'd already been deceived by a woman he had loved. She would not add to his heartbreak.

He was looking at her now with undisguised lust in his eyes. After coming inside where the air was on, she felt a chill, and her nipples had reacted to the change in temperature. She wouldn't lie to herself: It wasn't entirely the chilly air that had done that. It was Decker.

Decker had moved closer. His thigh was touching hers. She inhaled sharply, and exhaled slowly. She trembled as he slipped his arm around her waist and pulled her against him. She threw her head back, and he kissed the hollow of her throat. His warm lips on her skin sent wanton currents of pleasure pulsing through her. Her body went limp. The throbbing between her legs was a sign of her sexual readiness. Yes, she was past ready. There was no mistaking he was ready, too. His rock-hard erection was proof of that. "One hundred and twenty days," he whispered. His hot breath was on her neck. "I adore you. Can't you see we're made for each other? Say you want me, Desi. Just say the word, and I'm yours."

"Oh, God," she breathed. He had backed her against the sink, and her dress hem was hiked up, exposing her thighs. She had kicked off her shoes somewhere between here and the patio. Now their lower bodies were pressed together, pelvis to pelvis, and it didn't take a great imagination on her part to know they fit well together. The only thing that separated them were a few thin layers of clothing, wet clothing.

Their eyes met, and the smoldering passion in his was her undoing. "I want you," she said, her voice so low she could barely hear it herself. "I want you so bad."

He didn't say a thing. He simply picked her up and started walking in the direction of her bedroom. She wrapped her arms around his neck. Her nervousness made her say, "I should warn you, I talk in my sleep. Sometimes I wake myself up singing."

"I snore when I'm overly tired," he said, not even breathing hard as he took the stairs. "And I used to sleepwalk when I was a kid, but I haven't done that in a while, so I think you're safe."

"It's been so long since I did this, I think I may have forgotten how," she continued.

"Baby, I'd be happy to give you a refresher course."

"When you asked me what I was thinking a minute ago," she confessed, "I was thinking of having children with you, a houseful. Doesn't that freak you out?"

He smiled at her. "I've already picked out names for our first two children, Thaddeus the third for the boy, and Verity, after my grandmother, for the girl, with your okay, of course. So no, that doesn't bother me."

"Your name is Thaddeus?" she asked, confused.

He laughed shortly. "I'm named after my dad, whose name is Thaddeus. Decker is what they started calling me when I was born. My dad said I was the only thing that could deck my mother. Apparently she had a hard time during the delivery because I was so big. I decked her, hence Decker. Get it?"

"You're so strange," she said, smiling lovingly at him.

"We're a perfect match."

Decker stood in the doorway of the bedroom with Desiree in his arms. The bedside lamp was on, and since the last time he'd seen her bedroom on that tour four months ago, he saw she had done a bit of redecorating. The drapes and the comforter were a deep forest green now instead of white. It was almost as if she was trying to make the atmosphere more appealing for a man. If so, that meant she had recently given seduction some thought. That notion pleased him.

He walked farther into the room and set her down at the foot of the bed. She looked up at him, her eyes dreamy. Even drenched, she was the most beautiful, desirable woman he'd ever known. He had known women who were just as beautiful, yes, but somehow with their beauty, they had acquired a meanness of spirit that made them ugly in spite of their outside appearance. Desiree was beautiful on the inside and the outside. He felt so lucky that she had finally stopped living in the past. Time was a terrible thing to waste, and they had wasted so much of it.

"I'd like to undress you," he said, his voice hoarse.

She nodded. He felt a slight tremor run through her body. He knew she was nervous. He was nervous, too. He wanted her first experience in years to be memorable in a good way. Tonight, he was going to make sure that tomorrow morning, when she opened her eyes, it would be with a huge smile on her face.

He pulled the sundress over her head. Then he didn't know what to do with it because it was wet. She must have seen the indecision in his eyes, because she took the dress and went to hang it on a hook in the adjacent bathroom. When she returned, her eyes had a determined cast to them.

She was wearing a slip that, on her, looked like sexy lingerie. Her fit, golden-brown body, muscles undulating beneath smooth skin, was the focus of his attention. He could not tear his eyes away. Her nipples were clearly outlined beneath the silken material, and he wanted to bury his face in her cleavage. But he stood there as she came to him and began unbuttoning his shirt. When she was done, she sultrily ran her hands over his chest, taking her time. Then she bent her head and kissed it. When she raised her head, she finally spoke: "You're beautiful."

Her words made him harden further. He was beautiful to her. It was more than he could have hoped for, having gone months believing she never thought of him, let alone desired him.

He grabbed her and kissed her hard. At first he thought he'd been too rough, but soon she was controlling the kiss and moaning with pleasure. When they came up for air, her eyes were fierce and passion-filled. She began undressing quickly. He followed suit, and soon they were both naked, not taking their eyes off each other for one second.

Now he could not stop staring, and his heart thumped with excitement, to say nothing of his member, which had hardened so much he knew he would be fully erect soon. They circled each other like fencers about to duel. He took the opportunity to observe her from all angles. Some people should be naked 24/7, and she was one of them. Her body was smoothly muscular, yet utterly feminine. Her skin was unmarred, except for a scar on her right thigh, an old injury he would ask her about later. Her breasts were full and natural, with nipples he wanted to taste right now, but he maintained control. He wanted to know where she was going with this sensual dance. He lowered his gaze to her vagina and was pleased to note she was natural there, as well. Her navel was lovely, and he realized he'd never seen her in a bikini or a midriff top before.

She was watching him as closely as he was watching her. A smile crinkled the corners of her warm brown eyes. Obviously she liked what she saw. Her gaze traveled downward, and he couldn't help feeling a little self-conscious. No man liked being judged by his size. He had nothing to feel insecure about, but still. Her smile broadened, and she launched herself at him. Taken by surprise, he fell backward onto the bed with her on top of him. She kissed him, and they rolled until he was on top. She opened her legs to him, and he almost lost control.

The intoxicating scent of her, the warmth of her naked skin against his, were making his plans for a night of slow, intense lovemaking seem like a pipe dream. But he was determined and redoubled his efforts. "Where are your condoms?" he asked before this could go any further.

"They're in the top drawer of the bureau," she said, and actually started to grind against him, the little devil.

He got up and looked in the drawer.

"I hope you haven't had these for ten years," he joked.

"No, silly, I bought them recently. I wanted to be prepared."

Finding a small box of condoms stuck in a corner, he opened it and withdrew a couple of packets. Returning to the bed, he put the condoms on the nightstand for easy access later, and straddled her.

He moved backward on the bed on his knees and then bent to lick her nipples, first one, then the other, taking his time and enjoying every minute of it. She rubbed his head, moaning loudly, modesty out the window. He smiled and moved down a bit more, his tongue exploring her navel next. She writhed with pleasure, which caused him to harden even more. He'd bet she didn't know until this moment that the navel was an erogenous zone. He wanted to know what she would think of what he intended to do to her next.

He got up, grabbed her gorgeous legs and pulled her toward the foot of the bed, after which he got on his knees and joked, "No sudden moves. I don't want you to take my head off."

Desiree laughed softly. "I'll try not to."

He felt her body relax as he coaxed her legs apart. She did offer a bit of resistance. He attributed this to her lack of knowledge about what was to come. Perhaps she'd never been pleasured in this manner before. In which case, she was in for a treat. He began by gently kissing the insides of her thighs. That was her initiation. When she was putty in his hands, he went for the gold and plunged his firm, hot tongue into her honey pot like a hungry bear.

"Oh, my God," she gasped, tensely at first, and then as she relaxed, she said again it with a note of rapture in her voice. He had a new convert.

She climaxed with a shudder. He didn't stop until he felt her release, although he did decrease the intensity, allowing her to float down from the precipice in a gentle manner.

The sound of her contented sigh was his reward.

He then got to his feet, his member hard as it had ever been. After putting on a condom, he pulled Desiree, who was still coming down from her high, forward and then he gently but thoroughly entered her. It felt so good he wanted to shout, but he restrained himself.

He waited a moment for her response. Her eyes fluttered open, and she looked at him in amazement; then she smiled, sighed and met his thrusts with as much energy and enthusiasm as he. Oh, yeah, this was going to be a good night.

Chapter 8

Desiree didn't remember sex being this much fun. Admittedly, she wasn't much of an expert. Noel had been her first and only, and in retrospect, he hadn't been very giving as a lover.

She rarely had one orgasm, let alone two with him. She'd been too naive back then to tell him her needs weren't being met.

She turned and grinned at Decker after they'd made love for the second time that night. They'd fallen back onto the bed, facing each other, exhausted. He was smiling, too, and his eyes were quite mellow as they lovingly regarded her. "How's the refresher course going?" he asked.

"Excellent, if I do say so myself," she returned happily.

"You're a fast learner."

"I've always been an overachiever."

He gently touched her cheek. His eyes raked over her face as though she were the most precious thing in the world to him. "I'm so sorry I wasted years behaving like an idiot. If I'd come to you correctly the day we met, we wouldn't have wound up wasting two years."

"It's not your fault," Desiree said. "I had a wall up around my heart. I probably wouldn't have been receptive to you if you *had* come to me correctly, as you put it. Let's face it, this is our time."

She loved the way his forehead crinkled when he frowned. "I don't want to sound ungrateful for this blessing, because I am. It's just that I can imagine how far we would be now if things had been different."

"Oh, no," Desiree said, laughing softly. "You're one of those what-might-have-been people."

"Hear me out," he said.

"I'm listening."

"Colton Jr. could have had a little cousin by now," he said. "And maybe we'd be working on number two. I'm thirty-four. I'd like children before I get decrepit."

Desiree laughed harder. "You're a young man. You take care of yourself. You still have plenty of years during which you can play ball with your son and daughter."

He laughed. "No daughter of mine is going to play sports. She'll be a little lady. I'm going to spoil her rotten."

Desiree sat up in bed, pulling the sheet over her chest as she did so. She glared at him. "If you really feel that way, you can get out of my bed right now, because no daughter of mine is going to sit on the sidelines. Playing sports and being active give a girl confidence. I'm going to sign my daughter up for martial arts as soon as she shows an interest. And any other sport she wants to play."

Decker was up on his elbow, still lying next to her, with a humorous expression in his dark gray eyes as he looked up at her. "You're adorable when you get mad. Your eyes flash. And you growl, did you know that?"

Desiree hauled off and hit him with a pillow. "I should have known you were pulling my leg, pretending to be a Neanderthal!"

Sitting up, Decker caught the pillow and pulled it out of her grasp. "Hey, enough violence, sweet cheeks. I give up. Our daughter can learn karate. Don't blame me if she beats up all the boys in class, though, if she takes after her mother."

Desiree had a killer comeback for him, but when she was about to deliver it, her stomach growled so loudly she let his comment slide. Decker looked at her stomach and burst out laughing. "We didn't get the chance to eat much before the storm broke," he said.

"And then you jumped my bones," Desiree said, climbing out of bed. "How about a quick shower and then we go downstairs and raid the kitchen?"

"Who jumped whose bones?" Decker asked, following her into the bathroom. "I think there was a mutual jumping of bones."

She tossed a saucy grin over her shoulder. "I shouldn't be held liable for anything. I was practically a virgin until you showed up."

"Baby, those were not the moves of a virgin," Decker countered. "More like a vixen!"

In the bathroom, she turned and smiled at him. She was happy to hear he'd enjoyed her. She'd been a little worried she wouldn't please him. "A vixen, huh?" she said, going up to him and pressing her body against his. "Say that again."

He held her face between his hands and looked deeply into her eyes. "I'm glad I have a strong heart, or you would have killed me."

Desiree grinned. "That's the sweetest thing anyone has ever said to me." Then she kissed him.

When they parted, she whispered, "I love you."

Decker's smile vanished. He grabbed her by the upper arms, a look of astonishment on his handsome face. He heaved a huge sigh of relief. "You love me?"

Desiree blinked back tears. She nodded. "I do. I think I have for a while now, before we started dating. It was Lauren who pointed out the possibility to me. I would act as if your attention was annoying, but the fact is, I looked forward to your notes and your phone calls, but I was too blind to recognize those feelings for what they were. And, too, all the times we saw each other at family gatherings, I would subconsciously be waiting for when you'd enter the room. And once you did, I'd exhale with relief. Yeah, I think it's safe to say I've wanted you for a long time. Does that surprise you?"

"Hell, yeah, it surprises me," Decker exclaimed. He hugged her tightly, then released her and held her at arm's length. "I want you to know that you can trust me with your heart, Desi. You completely own mine. I'll never let you down."

She tiptoed and kissed his cheek. "And I'll never let you down, either."

About two weeks later, on Wednesday morning, Decker walked into his outer office at the firm and greeted his assistant, Kym Johnson, a tall, plus-size African-American woman in her fifties. She was grinning, which should have tipped him off that something was wrong. Kym was a friendly woman, highly efficient and thoroughly professional, but she wasn't a grinner. She smiled occasionally; otherwise she had her nose to the grindstone running the office, and anyone who stood in the way of her doing that usually caught hell. He liked that about her. He could rest assured that Kym had his back in the office.

He stood in front of her desk, briefcase in hand, and stared at her. "What's the matter?"

"There's a surprise waiting for you in your office," she said coyly. Kym being coy unnerved him. It was the word *surprise* that made him let his guard down. His thoughts immediately went to Desiree. Could she be waiting for him in his office?

He eagerly walked into his office, expecting to find her there, but instead he found his ex, Yolanda, sitting behind his desk as though she owned the place.

It took him a moment to recover from the shock, and then he saw red. Jaw clenched, he bit out, "What are you doing here?"

She got up from behind the desk and walked around to prop her bottom on the corner of it. She was dressed to kill in what was undoubtedly a designer slack suit and stilettos. Her light brown eyes seductively raked over him. "Hello to you, too," she purred. "Don't be angry at your assistant. I charmed her."

"In other words, you lied to her to get in here," he said, moving around her to set his briefcase atop the mahogany desk.

She laughed. "Oh, Decker, can we please be friendly? I came all the way from California to see you."

He wasn't falling for her con job. "Why?"

"I need your help."

"What makes you think I would help you?"

"You're not still mad at me after five years, are you?" She actually looked hurt. She began walking toward him, her movements calculated for the most seductive effect. She was still using her sexuality to her advantage. He noticed she was coloring her naturally black hair red these days. She was a little on the thin side. But he supposed actresses had to toe the line where their weight was concerned.

"I don't waste time being mad at you," he said evenly. "In fact, I don't waste time thinking about you at all."

"Don't be cruel," she pleaded, lowering her lashes

seductively and pouting. "Can't an old friend drop by to say hello?"

Decker had the satisfaction of realizing that he was immune to her. He glanced at his watch. "I have an appointment in five minutes. That should be sufficient time for us to reminisce. So if you really have something important to say, you'd better get to saying it."

She stuck her bottom lip out like a child about to throw a tantrum and pushed herself up from the desk. Then she dropped the seductive act and got down to business, looking him in the eye. "I need your help, Decker. My cousin is in trouble. He's been languishing in jail for months now on trumped-up charges. He's not cooperating with the public defender. He's so despondent that recently he stopped eating. I'm afraid he's going to starve himself to death if I can't offer him some hope. You're the best defense attorney in town. Please help him!"

Decker thought her words had the ring of truth to them, but he still had to be cautious. She had proven herself to be untrustworthy in the past. There was no reason to believe she'd changed. "What's his name? And what's he charged with?"

"Frederic Sawyer. He's a teacher, and one of his female students claims he had sex with her."

"Did he?"

Her eyes were alarmed. "Of course not," she cried indignantly. "He's not an animal. He's been teaching at that school for over a decade. The students love him. Everyone is rallying around him. These accusations will ruin his career."

"It wouldn't be the first time a child molester was found working in an occupation that brings him in daily contact with the object of his obsession. Are you sure your cousin's innocent?"

"We grew up together, Decker. I know him. He's a family man. He would never harm a child. Please, just go speak with him. I'm begging you!" Tears welled in her eyes.

Decker sighed. He, like most men, had a low tolerance for women's tears. "I'll go see him," he said. "But that's all I'm promising."

"Thank you, thank you, thank you so much!" she said, grasping his arm in appreciation. But Decker walked over to the door and held it open for her instead.

"When will you go see him?" she asked as she paused to look up at him.

"Soon," he said. "Now, if you don't mind, I really do have an appointment."

"All right," she said, disappointment mirrored in her perfectly made-up eyes. "Goodbye, Decker."

He closed the door and paced his office for a few minutes, wondering if fate was playing some sort of sick sadistic trick on him, bringing the woman who'd ripped his heart out back into his life shortly after he'd found love with his dream woman.

And the way Yolanda had behaved, as if she'd been willing to seduce him into representing her cousin. That was messed up!

* * *

Decker didn't get the chance to go see Frederic Sawyer until the following afternoon. He was well-known at the Raleigh Detention Center and had no problem getting in to talk to the teacher.

One of the detention staff brought Sawyer into the room that was used for lawyer-inmate confabs. Decker had been waiting for about half an hour. He was used to the wheels of justice turning slowly.

He didn't know how thin Sawyer had been before his arrest, so he had nothing with which to compare the emaciated man he saw before him. Decker, being human, was immediately sympathetic.

"Mr. Sawyer, my name is Decker Riley. I'm a lawyer, and your cousin Yolanda asked me to come see if I can help you."

Sawyer appeared too tired to even raise his bowed head.

"Mr. Sawyer, do you understand how serious your situation is? You could go to prison for the rest of your life. Do you even care? Because if you're so far gone that you have no fight left in you, then I'm wasting my time."

Frederic Sawyer raised his head and looked at Decker. "I have nothing to live for. My wife left me and took my kids with her. My life is over."

"Where did she go?"

"Huh?"

"Your wife," Decker said. "Where did she take your kids?"

"To her parents' place in Terre Haute," Sawyer said in a monotone.

"That's a ten-hour drive from here," Decker said, hoping to get Sawyer to open up. "Why do you think she did that?"

"Because she thinks I'm guilty, and she wants to put as much distance between us as possible."

"Didn't you tell her you were innocent?"

"I tried, but she wouldn't listen. I told her Madison made it up because she's obsessed with me. I never touched that girl!"

"How long have you known Madison? What's her last name?"

"It's Samuelson. I've known her since the beginning of the school year. She's in my sixth-period trigonometry class. She's also the class aide."

"She must be pretty smart, taking trig," Decker said, his tone easy.

"She's one of my best students. I was very fond of her until she accused me of raping her."

"Have you ever been accused of anything like that before?" Decker had thought it a harmless question until Sawyer changed right before his eyes.

His eyes were black orbs of hate when he turned his gaze on Decker. He leaned across the table and bared his teeth like a wild animal. Spit came out of his mouth when he demanded menacingly, "Who have you been talking to? Yolanda didn't send you. Get the hell out of here!"

That was when Decker knew he was guilty. Sawyer had gone from docile to vicious in a matter of seconds. Decker would bet that the Samuelson girl wasn't his first victim. He intended to find out. The problem with police investigations was that cases were often assigned to overworked individuals who didn't have the time to turn over every rock looking for evidence. The authorities would prosecute Sawyer, but they would do it based on one girl's testimony, testimony that might easily be refuted by a talented defense attorney.

Sawyer continued to regard him with a baleful stare. The hate that radiated off the man was palpable. Decker felt he was in the presence of evil. Sawyer might well be insane. That was something a psychologist would have to determine. But even if he was insane, he would still be punished to the full extent of the law for what he had done to the Samuelson girl.

"I don't want you on my case," Sawyer said through clenched teeth. "I don't want you anywhere near me. And stay away from my wife."

"You take care, Mr. Sawyer," Decker said casually as he got up to leave.

Yolanda didn't know it, but she'd just made sure her cousin would spend the rest of his life in prison. Decker walked swiftly through the detention center to the part of the building that housed the police department.

Ten minutes later, he had tracked down the lead detective on the Sawyer case and was sitting across from him in his tiny cubicle. He explained that he'd been asked by a relative of Sawyer's to go see him with the prospect of representing him. "Have you spoken with Mrs. Sawyer yet?" was his first question.

"Yes, but she wasn't very helpful to us. She seemed to be focused on protecting her children. What good parent wouldn't?" Detective Antonio Diaz's eyes scanned his computer screen for a moment. "Two little girls, ages seven and four, it says here."

"Girls, huh?" Decker said contemplatively.

"I know what you're thinking," Diaz said. "You're thinking he may have molested his own children. But if his wife was aware of that going on, wouldn't she step forward and press charges?"

"You'd be surprised what some people try to hide for the sake of their privacy. If it were true, that kind of stigma could follow those girls for the rest of their lives. If their mother can shield them from that, she will."

"I suppose you're right," Diaz conceded. "What are you getting at, Mr. Riley?"

"May I ask who interviewed Mrs. Sawyer?"

"I did it myself," Diaz answered. "She said she knew nothing about Sawyer's relationship with the Samuelson girl."

"Did you know she took the girls to her parents' in Terre Haute?"

"Of course," Diaz said. "She mentioned she might be doing that to escape media scrutiny, which we understood. She and her girls aren't under investigation."

"Does it strike you as odd that she wouldn't stay

in town to offer moral support to her husband, even if she sent her daughters to stay with her parents?"

Diaz paused to think about that. He looked Decker straight in the eye. "She may be distancing herself from him for a reason."

Decker smiled, glad that the detective had gotten his point. "I believe she knows something. And from the reaction I just got from Sawyer when I mentioned his wife, I believe he knows his wife may know more about him than he's comfortable with. I think he was glad she left town so fast."

"I think I'll be going to Terre Haute to speak with Mrs. Sawyer again," Diaz said.

Decker rose and offered the detective his hand. "Good luck, and please let me know how it goes. I'm interested in making sure Sawyer gets what he deserves."

Diaz chuckled as he rose and shook Decker's hand. "Then I guess you won't be taking his case."

"No, I won't," Decker said emphatically. "I have to at least entertain the notion of a client's innocence, and I don't get that feeling from Sawyer."

"Tell the truth, Petra," Desiree said as she and her sisters sat on the floor in front of the couch in Meghan's living room, drinking wine and eating popcorn. "You must get bored out of your mind living in the jungle with no other human for company!"

Petra laughed with gusto. She had long black curly hair, like her sisters, but unlike them, she hadn't cut hers in years, so it fell to her waist. "I don't have time to get bored, Desi. I survive in the jungle rather like the great apes do. I forage for food, and I'm constantly moving because they're constantly on the move, and I follow them. And I have to stay alert because they're aware of my presence, and not being able to predict what they'll do next, even after years of studying them, I have to worry that suddenly they're no longer going to tolerate me and get rid of the irritating human."

Desiree, Meghan, Lauren and Mina all looked horrified. "Have you ever been attacked?" Lauren asked. She had Colton Jr. in her arms. The toddler was sound asleep, his aunts having lavished attention on him all day, which tired him out. It was early evening now.

"No, never," Petra said. She had golden-brown skin like her sisters, but hers had been darkened a bit by the equatorial African sun. She wore no makeup, a habit she'd acquired over the years from the inadvisability of doing so in her line of work. As a zoologist whose specialty was the great apes, she made her workplace the great outdoors. "Once I got too close to a silverback—that's a mature alpha who's generally the leader of his group—and he beat the ground, letting me know he wasn't pleased about it. But I just stood still, keeping my gaze elsewhere because they don't like you to look them directly in the eyes. That's like a challenge to them. He soon lost interest in me and went back to foraging. Grubs were more interesting to him than I was."

"Are they aggressive by nature?" Desiree asked.

"I've only noticed aggression in the case of guarding against enemies daring to enter their territory, as I did, and males fighting other males for a choice female during mating season. Otherwise they're content to go about their business."

"What exactly is a choice female?" Desiree asked.

"Young, strong and capable of satisfying the imperative to survive—in other words, fertile," Petra answered with a smile. "You know, the same way human males pick females."

The sisters laughed at that. Desiree changed position on the floor, stretching her legs out and wiggling her toes. They were all dressed comfortably in jeans or shorts and T-shirts, and they were barefoot. "I've known some alpha males like that in my day," she said with a giggle.

"You're dating one right now," Lauren said.

"Decker's not an alpha. He's too sweet to be an alpha."

"Alphas can be sweet," Petra said. "But watch out if anyone threatens his woman. Then he's ferocious."

"I kind of like that," said Meghan dreamily. "Women these days have to do everything for themselves. It would be nice to have a man you can count on who can be your hero when you need him."

"That's Colton," Lauren said. She bent and kissed Colton Jr. on the forehead. In sleep, he looked angelic.

"When is my hero going to come along?" Meghan lamented, tossing her head back dramatically and sighing loudly.

Desiree smiled at her baby sister. "When you least expect it."

"Isn't that the truth?" Mina said. She reached up and pushed a long braid behind an ear. "None of us who are in relationships were looking for them. Maybe that's the secret—once you stop caring whether or not you meet a man, he shows up."

"In that case, I'm never going to meet anyone," Meghan said with a laugh. "I'm in love with the thought of being in love, possibly because I've never been in love."

"Believe me," Desiree said. "When it does finally happen, it'll be worth the wait. Sometimes when you wait a long time, you appreciate it more."

"I'm perfectly happy not being in love," Petra spoke up. "I know. Being in love is the ultimate goal of all red-blooded girls. But with it comes expectations, and I don't want any man expecting me to be at his beck and call. Or expecting me to bear his children and then take most of the responsibility of raising them from infancy to college age. Women get the short end of the stick in marriage. But because love, a mind-altering drug if there ever was one, is involved, women are brainwashed into believing they're happy in marriage."

Her sisters looked at her as though she had taken leave of her senses, and then burst out laughing.

"You've been in the jungle too long, girl," Lauren said. "We've got to find you an alpha male in a hurry."

"Uh-huh," Meghan agreed. "Like yesterday!"

"How long has it been since you kissed a guy?" Lauren asked.

Petra was smiling now. "I know my views aren't popular, but if married women were honest, they would agree with me. They give a hundred percent, and if their husbands give fifty, they're lucky."

"You just haven't found the right man," Lauren insisted.

But Desiree refused to try to talk Petra out of her beliefs. As a psychologist, she found her views refreshing. Petra, in her opinion, had always been observant about human behavior.

"Leave Petra alone," she said. "She's entitled to her views, and you know she's never sugarcoated anything. I agree that marriage can be much more advantageous to males than females. Women do expend more energy raising the children, maintaining the household, even managing their social lives. I hear everything in my practice. The biggest gripe among couples in couples therapy is that the marriage duties, or whatever you want to call the day-to-day chores couples share, are unequal. Women recognize they're working themselves too hard, and men seem to be oblivious of that fact." She smiled at Petra. "But as for giving up on love, I could never do that. Love, to me, makes everything else worthwhile."

Petra smiled at Desiree. "Oh, I believe in love, I just don't believe in letting it rule my head."

"Back to my question," Lauren said. "When was the last time you kissed a guy?"

"If you must know," Petra said with a gleam in her eye, "I kissed a very handsome guy while I was in New York a few days ago. In fact, I did more than kiss him. I made love to him."

There were looks of astonishment on her sisters' faces at that statement. She smiled. "It was a huge mistake. I was lonely, and he, well I don't know why he did it."

"Have you looked in a mirror lately?" Meghan asked. "You're hot, sis!"

Petra laughed. "I don't know what hot is. I exist in khakis, and I usually smell like bug spray. Insects will pick you up and fly away with you in the jungle. But there was something about Chance Youngblood that got to me, and I ended up spending the night with him. Now I don't know how I'm going to look him in the eye the next time I see him."

"Oh, it's likely you're going to see him again?" Desiree asked.

"He's head of the network that wants me to star in a new reality series about my work," Petra said.

"Ooh, this is getting complicated." Meghan sighed. "Tell us more about this Chance Youngblood. What does he look like?"

Desiree smiled. Her baby sister was a die-hard romantic. She was surprised when the practical Petra looked dreamy before describing the man in question. "He's ruggedly handsome, which I think is what turned me on. I can't stand pretty boys. He's got this rough-and-tumble way about him. He moves like a panther and has the most beautiful dark brown skin. His body's hard, and he had plenty of stamina."

The sisters erupted in excited hoots and hollers once more. Colton Jr. stirred in his mother's arms and went right back to sleep.

"Which he had to have to keep up with me," Petra continued just for the shock value, Desiree suspected.

Desiree laughed. "There's something to be said for good stamina."

"You two are so bad," Meghan said. "And here I haven't had a man in my bed for nearly three years."

Suddenly Desiree cried, "Meghan, turn that up!"

Meghan, who was closest to the TV's remote on the coffee table, reached over and turned the volume up on the evening news.

On the screen, Yolanda Reynolds was being interviewed by the local TV station's entertainment reporter.

Chapter 9

"Who is that?" Petra asked, frowning.

"Yolanda Reynolds," Desiree replied coldly.

"Yolanda Reynolds? I know I've heard that name before. You mean that girl who used to pick on you in school?" Petra said, confused. "What's she doing on TV?"

In answer, the reporter beamed at Yolanda and asked, "Is there a particular reason you're visiting your hometown, Yolanda? Not that we wouldn't be delighted to have you back under any circumstances!"

Yolanda, a seasoned professional, smiled warmly at the reporter and said, "I'm here to offer moral support to my cousin, Frederic Sawyer. As you know, he finds himself in a bit of a jam right now."

"A bit of a jam is not what he's in," Desiree cried. "The man's accused of molesting a fifteen-year-old girl!"

"I take it you're familiar with the case," Petra said.

"Yes, the girl he's accused of molesting is a patient of mine," Desiree stormed, getting to her feet and pointing at the TV screen. "And that snake is using her popularity to try to garner support for him."

"I don't understand," Petra said. "Is she supposed to be some kind of celebrity? She's preening like a she-ape in heat."

Desiree couldn't help it. She laughed at Petra's comment. "She's an actress," she explained. "She's had a few hit movies, and she stars in the highest-rated show on TV." She sat back down beside Petra and took deep breaths in an effort to calm herself. She just hoped Madison wasn't somewhere watching one of Raleigh's most famous hometown girls talking about her cousin as if he were the victim in this whole scenario.

"I don't watch much TV," Petra said. "All I remember about her is that she was mean to you."

The program moved on to another segment, and Meghan muted the volume once more. "Does anyone want some real food?" she asked. "This popcorn isn't doing a thing for me. Who wants to order Chinese?"

The others discussed what they wanted from the menu while Desiree sat quietly, thinking about Yolanda Reynolds's presence in Raleigh. She claimed she was in town to support her cousin in his time of need. What her cousin needed most was a sharp lawyer who was an ace in the courtroom. Desiree could think of only one man who fit that description.

"Excuse me," she said to her sisters as she went looking for her handbag, which she'd left somewhere upstairs. "I have to make a phone call."

"Now I guess I'm one of you," Decker joked as he looked around the table at Colton, Juan and Will. "All wrapped up in a woman and happily whipped."

He had to talk loud to be heard over the cacophony of the bustling bar on Glenwood Avenue.

They laughed at him. Tall, lanky Will shook his bald head sympathetically. "Yeah, what a difference a few months make, huh? You're no longer lonely and pathetic. I can tell you now. I was beginning to worry about you."

"Yeah," Juan agreed heartily, "I thought you'd stay delusional for the rest of your life."

"Delusional?" Decker asked, curious.

"Believing that you were happy dating one beautiful woman after another instead of falling in love with one great woman," Colton explained. "Hey, I thought like that, too, until Lauren blew my mind."

Decker's cell phone rang, and he checked who was calling. "Got to take this," he said. "Excuse me." He rose to walk to the back of the bar, where it was a bit quieter.

"Hey, babe," he said to Desiree. He smiled, imagining her beloved face. "Enjoying your time with the girls?"

"Yes, we're talking up a storm and catching up,"

Desiree said. He could hear the smile in her voice. "Sweetie, listen, I thought you should be forewarned. I just saw Yolanda on the local news. She's back in town, and you'll never guess why she's here."

"She's trying to help her cousin avoid jail on molestation charges," Decker said calmly.

He heard Desiree's sharp intake of breath. "Then she's been to see you," she said with a note of caution in her tone, which he found a bit disturbing. Why would she feel she had to tread carefully with him?

"Yes, she asked me to go see her cousin. His name's Frederic Sawyer, he's a high school teacher and he's in jail on charges that he seduced one of his students."

"I know," Desiree said. "The girl is the same patient I mentioned to you."

"Oh, no," Decker cried, shocked. "Not the girl who's now being harassed at school because she stood up for herself?"

"Yeah. Small world, isn't it?"

"I'm sorry, I had no idea," Decker said sincerely.

"I know you didn't," Desiree sighed. "Please tell me you're not thinking of defending that man, Decker!"

"No, baby, I'm not going to take the case. But I did give the lead detective some advice that will hopefully help convict Sawyer. That's the extent of my involvement. I'm very interested in the outcome, though. I asked the detective to keep me in the loop."

"I'm so relieved," Desiree said. "When I heard Yolanda talking about her cousin on TV and how she was here to support him in any way she could, I had a gut feeling she was going try to convince you to represent him." Decker wished he were with her so he could hold her. Then she'd know that she had nothing to worry about.

"She gave it her best shot," Decker said. "But baby, didn't I tell you I'd never let you down?"

"Yes," she said softly.

"You do believe me, don't you?"

"Yes, I do," she said without hesitation.

He breathed a sigh of relief. "Good, because there is nothing I wouldn't do for you."

"I wish I could see you tonight," she said. Her tone had a haunting lilt to it, which made him again want to hold her.

"Tonight is for your sisters," he told her with a smile. "Tomorrow night, after your parents' anniversary party, you're mine."

"You can count on it," she said, and he heard that smile again.

"I love you," he said with feeling.

"I love you," she replied, her voice husky with emotion, "more each day."

Desiree went back downstairs and rejoined her sisters, sitting on the floor beside Mina, but she couldn't shake the feeling that Yolanda was not only in town to show support for her cousin, but to wreak havoc in her relationship with Decker.

Meghan was on the phone ordering takeout. "Desi, you want shrimp-fried rice, right?" she asked.

"Sure, that'll be fine," Desiree replied halfheartedly.

Mina turned and smiled at her. "What's wrong?"

Desiree looked into Mina's face. Mina had been sitting cross-legged on the floor. She stretched out her jeans-clad legs and regarded Desiree with a curious expression.

Out of the corner of her eye, Desiree saw Meghan hang up the phone, and come back to sit among the rest of them. Desiree didn't have to look up to know all eyes were on her. They were so close, they shared an almost psychic connection.

The room was quiet now except for the sound of Colton Jr.'s breathing as he slept on the couch where his mother had placed him a few minutes ago.

"I'm afraid to voice my fears," Desiree began, "because it'll sound as if I don't trust Decker, and I do."

"Is this about Yolanda?" Lauren asked. "Do you think she's going to make a play for Decker?"

Petra looked confused. "Why would Yolanda try to seduce Decker?"

"Decker used to be in love with her," Desiree explained.

"You guys need to fill me in!" Petra cried.

"Long story short, she used him and tossed him aside when she got her big break. He was bitter about it, but he's come to terms with it now and considers himself lucky she dropped him when she did," Desiree told her.

"Okay, then," said Mina. "You have nothing to

worry about. Decker wouldn't touch that harpy with a ten-foot pole."

"You're right," Desiree said. "Decker won't touch her, but what about her touching him? You've seen her. Men can't resist her."

"Not all men are incapable of controlling their impulses," Petra said. "They can be faithful if they want to be. I don't buy the fallacy that all men are dogs. We have two examples of faithful men in our own family, Grandpa Beck and Daddy."

"How do you know Daddy never cheated on Mama?" Meghan asked, being the Devil's advocate.

"He's still breathing, isn't he?" Mina said with a laugh. "Virginia Beck-Gaines wouldn't stand for it."

"Oh, you'd be surprised by what married women have put up with to keep their marriages intact," Desiree said. "I've counseled couples after husbands have cheated. And I've heard the same thing from wives every time. While in theory, they had believed they couldn't live with their husbands if they'd cheated on them, they actually didn't know how they would react until it happened to them. Then they learned that if they really loved their husbands and they weren't serial cheaters, they could find it in their hearts to forgive them."

"Back to your problem, though," Lauren said. "Why are you having misgivings? Is it because Noel cheated on you? Because if it is, remember, Desi— Decker isn't Noel. I've seen the change in Decker over the years since he's been in love with you. And I say this because I believe he's been in love with you much longer than recently. Did you know he stopped dating anyone a full year or more before you went out with him? I got this straight from Colton, whom Decker confides in."

"I think part of my insecurity stems from Noel's cheating, yes," Desiree confirmed. "But I believe most of it is because I've never been able to sustain a long-lasting relationship. And I really want this one to last."

"And it will," Mina assured her. She hugged her. "I know having faith in someone is hard to do, but you've just got to let go, Desi, and believe that Decker would rather cut off his right arm than hurt you."

"Yeah," Lauren agreed. "Speaking as the other married woman in the room, I have to say that without faith in your partner, you might just as well hang it up. It's a waste of time and energy worrying that he's going to cheat on you. Because, let's face it, you can't watch him 24/7. The thought of doing that is exhausting! There are good men in the world, Desi, and Decker's one of them."

After a group hug, Desiree felt so much better. She resolved to put aside her petty fears and live in the moment, with the fervent belief that love would always bring Decker home to her.

Detective Diaz's cab pulled up to the Sneed residence in a middle-class neighborhood in Terre Haute the next day around noon.

Carla Sawyer was expecting him. They had spoken on the phone, and when he had told her he had further questions he needed to ask her, after which he wouldn't be bothering her again, she'd sounded relieved and had agreed to speak with him.

The woman who answered the door obviously wasn't Carla Sawyer. She was in her sixties.

After Detective Diaz introduced himself, she smiled and said, "Come in, Detective. I'm Carla's mother, Lydia Sneed."

She directed him to the living room, where she gestured for him to sit on the well-worn couch. Then she turned away, saying, "I'll get Carla."

The next woman to enter the room was in her late twenties. She was thin with light brown skin and light brown eyes. Her hair was sandy brown, and she wore it in a short, choppy style. In her right hand she carried a thick black leather-bound book. She almost looked faded to Detective Diaz—wan, withdrawn and in need of a good meal. He instinctively knew her appearance was probably due to worry over the events of the past few weeks. His heart went out to her.

He rose as she approached the couch, but she waved away his gentlemanly gesture. "Please sit down, Detective."

He sat back down, and she joined him on the couch and turned toward him. "I think I know why you're here," she said. She looked into his eyes. "I've been giving our last conversation a lot of thought, and I regret not being more forthcoming with you. You want to know if Freddy ever tried anything with our daughters. The answer is no, I don't think so, and I put it like that because the girls both deny that their father ever touched them inappropriately, but they adore their father, Detective Diaz. He always doted on them, spoiling them at every opportunity. But I'm still worried that as the years pass, they will remember something, something awful. There were times I'd wake up in the middle of the night, and he would be in their bedroom, watching them. I wonder now if he was tempted, but had managed to restrain himself from doing anything as vile as molesting his own children. It's a terrible thing not being able to trust your husband anymore, Detective."

On the one hand, Detective Diaz was relieved to hear that Sawyer, to the best of his wife's knowledge, had not touched his children. On the other, it sounded as though Carla Sawyer had nothing to go on except her suspicions.

She must have read the disappointment on his face, because she smiled and said, "But I do have something that I think will help your case."

She handed him the leather-bound book. He accepted it and opened it. It was a journal. More specifically, it was Frederic Sawyer's journal.

"I took this with me when I left Raleigh," Carla said. "He kept it locked in his desk drawer. I, of course, knew where he kept the key. I took it with me because I thought it might help if I had to blackmail him for him to leave me and the kids alone. I read it and wept."

Detective Diaz started reading at the beginning. It was a daily journal of his seduction of Madison

Samuelson. He wrote that she had "the disease to please," a characteristic he said many young girls had. They were trained, he theorized, to always want to please those around them. Therefore, they were easily influenced.

He read on, and the more he read, the more sickened he got. Sawyer had recorded for his reading pleasure every detail of how he had raped Madison the first time. Afterward he had convinced her that she had seduced *him*. How her beauty had been too powerful for him to resist. He pointed out that if she hadn't wanted to be with him, she would have screamed when he began pulling her clothes off. But she hadn't screamed.

That was all Detective Diaz had to see. He raised his eyes to Carla's. "You know what this means, don't you? He's going to prison, not to a psychiatric ward."

"Good," said Carla. She narrowed her eyes. "I've heard they don't like child molesters in prison."

"Let's hope he has the decency to confess after he learns the prosecutor has this journal."

"I hope so, too," Carla said. "I pray for that. I'm hoping he'll confess and save the taxpayers a trial, and save poor Madison from having to sit in court and relate all the things he did to her. She shouldn't have to go through that."

"My feelings exactly," Detective Diaz said, getting to his feet.

Carla rose and shook his hand. "Good luck, Detective. And if by chance you speak with Yolanda Reynolds, tell her for me that all the support in the world isn't going to change her cousin into a decent man. I saw what she did, trying to use her fame to curry favor for him. News travels fast over the internet. If he'd gotten the help he needed earlier in life, maybe I wouldn't have inadvertently married a molester, and my children wouldn't have to be going through this now!" She smiled sadly. "I know his family isn't to blame for what he is. People like him hide in plain sight. But I'm mad right now, and I want to blame somebody. I'll get over it eventually."

"Under the circumstances," Detective Diaz said, "you're coping surprisingly well."

On Saturday night guests began spilling into the ballroom at a luxury hotel in Raleigh. Desiree, along with Lauren, Mina and Meghan, was there to greet them. All pretense of a surprise party had been thrown out the window. Their mother, Virginia, had long since snooped out their plans. She and their dad, Alphonse, both resplendent in evening clothes, stood beside them and greeted the guests.

Alphonse, a tall, medium-brown-skinned, dignified retired army general, was, thanks to adhering to a slightly modified military workout schedule, in good shape. He bent his bald head and kissed the cheek of the upturned face of his petite wife, Virginia, the most beautiful girl in the world, Desiree had heard him say more times than she could count over the years. Virginia stood five feet two inches, and was trim from never being able to sit still for long. She had golden-brown skin, a trait all of her daughters had inherited, along with her abundance of coal-black hair, which now had silver streaks in it.

"Don't you think all of the guests have arrived by now?" she whispered to Desiree, who was standing next to her. "My feet are killing me in these pointy-toed torture devices better known as new shoes."

Desiree smiled. "Sure, Mama, you and Daddy can go sit down, or get on the dance floor. Somebody's got to get this party started."

"We'll leave that up to you children," her dad said, and took his bride by the hand and escorted her to their table.

Desiree surveyed the room. Over a hundred people were here, milling about chatting with each other, partaking of the appetizers offered up by the wait-staff (supper was to be served later) and frequenting the bars on opposite ends of the ballroom. The disc jockey had set up his equipment and speakers on the stage in the center of the room, and in front of the stage was the dance floor. Surrounding the stage and dance floor were tables, which she noticed some of the guests were already staking claim to.

"Excuse me, sis," Meghan whispered in her ear. "But I think your date has arrived."

Desiree looked up and saw Decker entering the ballroom. She sighed. The man was the epitome of style in his tuxedo. He saw her, raised an eyebrow in that cocky way he had and smiled, showing strong white teeth and dimples in his square-chinned face.

"You're drooling," Meghan joked, and playfully shoved her in Decker's direction.

Desiree didn't need further prodding. She hurried over to her man and hugged him. She hadn't seen him in more than twenty-four hours. Twenty-four hours during which she couldn't touch him. God, how she'd missed him. When his strong arms went around her now, she sighed and wondered how she'd ever lived without him.

When they parted, Decker said, "Hey, baby, you look stunning."

He took a step back, admiring her in the clinging red sheath dress with shirred sides. The bodice displayed just enough cleavage not to be scandalous, and the hem fell three inches above her knees. Desiree had worn her favorite pair of black Louboutin pumps. The red of the dress and the red soles of the shoes were a perfect match.

"Lady in red," Decker intoned as he pulled her into his arms again and, this time, kissed her lips briefly. When he raised his head, he said, "I've got good news. Detective Diaz told me his trip to Terre Haute was fruitful. Sawyer's wife provided some very compelling evidence that might prove his downfall. That's all I can tell you. I hope you understand."

Desiree was gazing at him with an expression of awe. "You're my hero."

He grinned. "That's all I ever wanted to be. Let's dance."

Aretha Franklin's "I Never Loved a Man (the Way I Love You)" was filling the ballroom with her soulful, gutsy voice.

Desiree sang along with the Queen of Soul as

Decker pulled her into his arms. "You're a no-good heartbreaker. You're a liar, and you're a cheat."

Decker bent and rubbed his cheek against hers. "Damn, you're sexy when you're singing. Nice voice, too. Will you sing to me later?"

Desiree grinned up at him. "Now, Decker, you know I'm not going to have the breath to waste on singing."

Pressed together like this, she could feel him growing erect right there on the dance floor. "I'm sorry," she teased. "Did I say something provocative?"

"God, I love you," Decker said, and held her closer.

Desiree laid her head on his shoulder and closed her eyes. "I missed you so much."

"It's only been twenty-four hours," Decker said softly.

"Twenty-four very long hours," she cooed.

Across the ballroom, sitting at a table with her date, Andre Hanks, Meghan scanned the room for Leo. She had personally invited him, telling him to bring a date. She smiled at Andre, a football coach at a local college. She and Andre had gone to college together and had dated off and on, but she had never been able to entirely trust him. He'd been a popular athlete in college and a chick magnet. Now they were each other's plus one at functions they didn't want to attend alone. There was an understanding between them: no sex. Andre was interested, but Meghan knew she couldn't trust him. Besides, he knew, and she knew, that he wasn't ready for a serious relationship. He was twenty-eight and far from being tired of sowing his wild oats.

Meghan had to admit, though, that Andre was prime man candy. If anyone could make Leo jealous, Andre would. Six-five, with muscles for days and a face so pretty that women literally tripped over themselves trying to get a closer look. Meghan had already spotted several women eyeing him this evening.

At last, her patience was rewarded, and Leonidas Wolfe (no wonder he insisted everyone call him Leo) strode into the ballroom with an attractive sister on his arm. Meghan sighed. She'd been hoping he wouldn't bring a date, but no matter. She was going to set her plan into action anyway.

She rose and reached back for Andre's hand. "Come on, I want to introduce you to someone."

Andre rose to his impressive height and rolled his powerful shoulders. Meghan pulled him across the room until they were standing in front of Leo and his date.

Meghan was pleased to see Leo's date's mouth fall open slightly as she perused the magnificent specimen that was Andre.

"Hi, Leo," Meghan said with enthusiasm. "I'm so glad you could come. This is my date, Andre Hanks. Andre, this is Leo Wolfe. His brother, Jake, is married to my sister Mina."

"Oh, yeah," Andre said. "The other twin." He vigorously pumped Leo's hand. Leo worked the kinks out of it after Andre let go of him.

"Hello, Andre, nice grip," he joked. Then he turned to his date. "Meghan Gaines, this is Shari Dunbar. Shari teaches English literature at Duke. Shari, this is my friend Meghan."

"Oh, yes," said Shari with a smile. Meghan guessed Shari was in her midthirties. She was of average height and had dark brown curly hair, which she wore in an upswept style for the evening. Meghan admired the clean lines of her off-white A-line dress. It suited her trim figure. She was prepared to like her until Shari continued speaking. "The history instructor who looks more like a student than an instructor. It's a pleasure to meet you, Meghan."

Shari's description of her rankled (was that how Leo saw her?), but Meghan forced a smile and said, "Welcome, Shari. I hope you enjoy yourself this evening. Excuse me, won't you? I think my sister's trying to get my attention."

Actually Desiree *was* beckoning her from across the ballroom. Meghan supposed it was time to take the stage, say a few words of welcome to the guests and bring out the surprise the sisters had in store for their parents.

She once again grabbed Andre by the hand and dragged him across the ballroom.

Secreted away in an alcove in the lobby of the hotel where the anniversary party was taking place, Petra sat on an overstuffed chair and grimaced down at her cell phone. She'd just received another text from Chance Youngblood.

Where R U?

Y do U want 2 know?

Must talk 2 U face 2 face.

I'll B back in NY in 2 wks.

I can't wait that long.

U have 2.

Y did you run away?

Because I didn't want 2 face U, isn't that obvious?

Just tell me where U R.

Frustrated with his incessant questions, she decided to tell him exactly where she was. What good would the information do him? He was in New York City. She wasn't staying at this hotel. She was only going to be here for a couple of hours.

When she was finished she texted, R U satisfied?

Not yet, but soon.

That last text puzzled her, but she didn't have time

to reflect on it because Desiree was phoning her. She answered, "It's time?"

"Yes, come to the ballroom. When you hear the song, come inside."

Chapter 10

"Welcome, everyone, to the thirty-fifth anniversary celebration of our parents' wedding," Lauren said with a warm smile directed at the guests standing in front of her and her sisters, who were on the raised stage. "I'm the eldest, Lauren. Every year we try to surprise our parents, but every year we fail because our mother is the nosiest woman in the tri-state area, and nothing gets past her!"

Waves of good-natured laughter swept through the ballroom.

Desiree stepped up to the microphone. "So this year we decided to do something different. Mom and Dad, come on up here."

The guests applauded, encouraging Alphonse and Virginia to join their daughters onstage. Once they were onstage, Virginia quipped, "Oh, goodie, it's time for presents." She looked at her daughters expectantly. The girls held out their empty hands, denoting there were no gifts forthcoming.

"Darn," said Virginia.

It was Mina's turn to speak. "Mom, Dad, you both have learned to live with loved ones' absences over the years. Dad, as an army general, you spent many years stationed abroad. Most of the time, Mom, you went with him, but later, you chose to stay in the States and raise us by yourself. Then, when I joined the army, you had to put up with my being away for months at a time. In recent years we've had to celebrate holidays without Petra, who's been in Africa for three years."

"That's my little Tarzan," Alphonse said with a smile. Desiree thought his eyes looked glassy at the mention of his daughter, whom he hadn't seen since Lauren's wedding two years ago.

The guests laughed at his comment, and Desiree felt compelled to explain their father's nickname for Petra. "You see," she said, "when Petra was a little girl she loved to read the Edgar Rice Burroughs's Tarzan adventures. Aside from the blatant racism she found in the pages, which she complained about, she loved the stories about animals, especially how the apes were depicted. This led to an interest in zoology. Today, our Petra is a zoologist studying the great apes in Central Africa."

Mina picked up the narrative. "Petra couldn't be

here today, Mama and Daddy, but we thought we'd play a song to remind you of her."

Hearing his cue, the disc jockey began playing "The Lion Sleeps Tonight." The song started with the very recognizable South African harmonies and then the words "In the jungle, the mighty jungle…"

At that point, Petra strode into the room, decked out in a beautiful black and gold African-print caftan, head-wrap and gold high-heeled sandals, dramatically declaring, "Mama and Daddy, did you know this song was written by the great South African Zulu musician Solomon Popoli Linda? It was a hit in South Africa long before various other musicians all over the world started covering it!"

Their mother screamed, "Petra, my baby girl!"

"I thought *I* was your baby girl," Meghan joked.

Desiree laughed. She had never seen her parents move so fast before. They were off the stage in no time hugging Petra, who was hugging them back and grinning widely.

The guests erupted in raucous laughter and applause.

Desiree gave the rest of her sisters hugs, in turn. "We got her!" she crowed. "It was a knockout. Virginia Gaines is down for the count."

Later, at supper, Desiree counted her blessings. It had been a long time since all of her sisters were at a family function together. She looked at everyone sitting at tables that had been shoved together to accommodate everyone.

Her parents were seated side by side, looking extremely pleased, and next to them were her grandpa Benjamin and her stepgrandma Mabel. Decker sat beside her, and his parents, June and Tad, were on his left, along with his aunt Veronica, Colton's mother. Then there was Lauren with Colton, Mina with Jake, and Jake's brother, Leo, with his date (whom she didn't know), Meghan and her date, Andre (she wondered how Meghan was taking the fact that Leo was dating someone) and Petra, who seemed perfectly fine with being dateless tonight.

"Okay, you got me," their mom suddenly announced. "Next year you won't be so lucky, I assure you."

"Mom," Mina said with a smile. "This time next year you're going to be a grandmother twice over."

Virginia shot up out of her chair and ran and threw her arms around Mina's neck. "The surprises never end."

Desiree and the girls joined their mother and took turns hugging Mina. "She even got us!" Desiree cried joyfully.

The men offered Jake congratulatory handshakes and pats on the back. Jake and Mina were all smiles after the congratulations as they stood with their arms around each other's waists. "We just found out last week," Jake said, looking lovingly into his bride's eyes. "We couldn't be happier."

"You know, I would be a tiny bit happier if it were twins," Virginia said hopefully. "Twins do run in your family."

"That's a possibility," Jake said, grinning. "But I'd be perfectly happy with a little girl who looks just like Mina."

"Let's not rule out having another boy," Benjamin put in. "The girls outnumber the boys in this family something fierce!"

To which everybody laughed.

"Grandpa," Mina said, "I'll see what I can do."

After supper, couples got up and danced. Petra was left at the table with Veronica Riley, Lauren's mother-in-law, whom she'd met at Lauren and Colton's wedding. She knew that Veronica was a widow who had recently reentered the dating life. Petra admired her style. She had dark brown hair with honey-blond streaks in it, and the short cut nicely framed her pretty face. In a matter of minutes, she had Petra laughing out loud at some of her experiences with men.

"At my age," Veronica, who was in her early sixties, said, "you've got to date men who're younger than you are. Men my age don't have the energy to date. I went out with this gentleman barely in his seventies after being introduced to him by my pastor. He wanted to go to dinner at five o'clock because he went to bed at eight. Plus, he no longer drove at night because of night vision problems, poor thing, so we couldn't plan anything after nightfall. We ended up going to a matinee, after which we hit the buffet at the Golden Corral, where he complained about the exorbitant prices, so I paid for my share. Then, after he brought me back home, he wanted to come in for a drink or coffee, but I looked up at the sky and said, "Oh, my, I think it's going to be sundown soon. You'd better hurry home before you can no longer see how to get there."

Petra laughed until she cried. "Did you ever see him again?"

Veronica smirked. "Of course not," she said. "I conveniently lost his contact information. Honestly, Petra, I don't believe I'm ever going to meet a man who can set my heart aflutter like my Frank did. But I'm a social person, and I'm not ready to sit at home. I've met a couple of interesting prospects, both about ten years my junior, but I'm a bit reluctant about letting myself get serious about either of them. They're nice to date because they can keep up with me, but the idea of marriage to a younger man doesn't appeal to me."

"Why?" Petra asked. "You would be a great catch for any man lucky enough to get you. I don't understand why women don't marry younger men more often than they do."

"I don't know," Veronica began. "I think it has to do with life experiences. Frank and I had a lot in common. We grew up in the same era. We could talk about anything. Sometimes I'll comment on a certain topic, and the younger guy just looks at me blankly. He has no idea what I'm talking about. It's exhausting having to explain things time and time again."

Petra reached up to tuck some of her hair behind an ear and noticed she'd lost one of her gold hoop earrings. She'd bought them in Ghana from an artisan who had fashioned them from twenty-four-karat gold especially for her. Because they were the only souvenirs she'd brought back with her from her first trip to Africa, they were of sentimental value. Plus, she wasn't exactly a fashionista like Desiree, whose closet was packed with beautiful clothes and whose jewelry case was a veritable gold mine. She packed light and didn't own a great deal of jewelry.

"You've lost an earring," Veronica said, noticing. "Have you any idea where it might be?"

"No," Petra said regrettably. "I don't know when it went missing. It could be anywhere."

"You should retrace your steps," Veronica suggested.

Petra rose and picked up her clutch. "I think I will. Excuse me, Veronica."

"Sure, dear," said Veronica. "Good luck!"

Petra made for the exit, figuring she would start at the beginning, which meant she had to go downstairs to the lobby, keeping an eye out for the gold hoop along the way.

By the time she entered the lobby, she hadn't had any luck locating the earring. The beautiful high-ceilinged lobby with its marble floor and gleaming front desk was relatively empty this time of night, ten-thirty. Petra went to the alcove where she'd been sitting prior to being called to the ballroom by Desiree. She looked between the cushions of the overstuffed chair she'd sat in, and lo and behold, she found the earring wedged between the cushion and the back of the chair.

Flush with victory, she was about to return to the ballroom when a deep voice said from behind her, "There you are."

She spun around and there, not six feet away from her, stood Chance Youngblood. A look of consternation marred his handsome dark brown face. He was wearing jeans, a light blue short-sleeve pullover shirt and black leather motorcycle boots. She remembered he'd said he was an avid motorcyclist. She found herself stunned into silence. Plus, there was the oomph effect that had rendered her momentarily unable to do anything except admire the sheer male beauty of him. She supposed the look of shock on her face was a source of amusement for him, because he laughed.

"We have unfinished business, Dr. Gaines."

"What, how..." she sputtered, backing up and nearly tripping over a big, square coffee table.

Chance reached out and steadied her. "I was in Raleigh when I phoned you," he explained. "But I didn't know where you were staying. In New York, you only told me you were going to see relatives in Raleigh."

"I can't believe you're here!"

He smiled and removed his hand from her arm. Walking around the coffee table and taking a seat on the off-white designer leather couch, he looked up at her, his gaze confident. "I'm not a man to be trifled with. You owe me an explanation."

His getting comfortable on the couch had given Petra the chance to regain her equilibrium. She sat down across from him and regarded him with narrowed eyes. "I don't owe you anything. We didn't make any promises to each other. It was just sex."

"Oh, I see, you make it a habit of having sex with any convenient male you run into?"

"No, of course not," Petra hissed. "I've never done anything like that in my entire life!"

His eyebrows rose. "Then I guess that makes me special," he said sarcastically.

"You know," Petra said with equal sarcasm, "most guys would be happy to be let off the hook. *You* travel halfway around the country to get into an argument with me in the lobby of a Raleigh hotel."

"I'm not most men," Chance said. He sighed and got to his feet. "Look, can we go somewhere and talk about this? I have a car waiting."

"I can't go anywhere right now," Petra said irritably.

She got up, too. Sitting while he towered over her made her feel like a little girl getting reprimanded by an angry parent. "I'm here attending a family gathering. I'd have to go back to the ballroom and let one of my sisters know I'm leaving."

"No problem," said Chance. "I'll wait here until you return." He stood with his arms crossed, an immovable force.

Petra was indecisive, a state she wasn't often in. But Chance Youngblood had been able to unnerve her from the beginning. She was both attracted to him and appalled by him. He came from a family that had been wealthy for generations which, in her opinion, was the cause of his huge ego.

He was not used to anyone telling him no. His presence here was evidence of that.

She blew an exasperated breath between full lips and looked up at him. "You might just as well come with me. My sisters would never forgive me if they found out you were here and they didn't get the chance to meet you."

He gave her a smug smile. "You told them about me, huh?"

"Don't look so pleased," Petra said as they began walking in the direction of the ballroom. "I told them you were a one-night stand."

"But a memorable one-night stand," he wagered.

"Don't make me change my mind," Petra warned.

Meghan was returning from a visit to the ladies' room when she ran into Leo in the corridor adjacent to the ballroom. Her face grew hot with embarrassment when she saw him, and she diverted her gaze momentarily so that she could school her facial expressions. The last thing she wanted him to realize was that she still had feelings for him.

She recalled how hopeful she had been at Lauren and Colton's wedding when Leo seemed smitten with her. Then he'd backed off, saying he believed his being ten years her senior put her at a disadvantage, and she should see younger men. He'd made it sound as if he were doing the chivalrous thing. But she had suspected he simply wasn't attracted to her, which further confused her because every time they were in the same room she would catch him looking at her as if he wanted to drag her off to the nearest bed and make love to her. Was she reading him wrong?

"How's your evening going?" she asked conversationally.

Leo paused a moment. He looked at the retreating back of a man who was entering the ballroom. Then, apparently satisfied that they were alone, he focused his attention on her.

There was a lovesick feeling in the pit of her stomach. She wished she could stop physically reacting to his nearness, but it was a losing battle.

"Meghan, what are you doing with a guy like that?" Leo said softly as he bent close. His light brown eyes held a look of concern in them. "He's been checking out other women all night long. You deserve better than that!"

Meghan sighed, shaking her head. "Andre and I aren't exclusive. I know he plays the field."

"And you're okay with that?" he asked incredulously.

"I'm young, remember? I'm not mature enough for a serious relationship," she taunted him.

"That's not what I meant when I said you and I shouldn't date, and you know it," Leo said. He ran a hand over his head in an exasperated gesture.

He'd let his hair grow out. The first time she'd met him, his head was shaved. Now he had a full head of dark brown, wavy natural hair, cut close to his scalp. She wanted to run her hand over it again and again. But then, there were many things she would never do with Leo.

"It doesn't matter what you meant, Leo, because the result is the same—I want you, and you don't want me." Meghan hadn't meant to say that, but she was mad, and it had felt good to say it!

"When I'm forty, you'll be thirty," Leo said as he held her gaze. "When I'm eighty and senile, you'll still be beautiful at seventy."

"What about now?" Meghan cried. "Just tell me once and for all that you're not attracted to me, and that's the reason you won't date me. Say the words so I can hear and understand, because you confuse me, Leo. The way you look at me, it's so hot it makes my skin burn. It drives me crazy! Does that woman mean anything to you?" She'd tacked that last question on out of morbid curiosity. The thought of Leo touching another woman sickened her.

His eyes were suddenly panicked. "Shari's just an acquaintance." He looked away, sighed and returned his gaze to hers. "I have a heart problem, Meghan. It's serious. I could drop dead any minute. You don't need a man who may die on you. You deserve someone who's going to be with you for the long haul."

Meghan felt faint. Her legs went weak, and Leo had to grab her before she hit the floor. But then she was in his arms, and their bodies were touching.

"Are you all right?" he asked in that deep, rich baritone. She melted. Tears pooled in her eyes as she looked up at him, but in spite of his revelation, she felt her strength returning. She'd come from generations of strong women, and they had never let something like illness keep them from the men they wanted. "It's too late for dire warnings, Leo Wolfe, because I'm completely in love with you."

Then he kissed her.

"What a night!" Desiree said with a laugh as she walked into her house with Decker following close behind. "You could have knocked me over with a feather when Chance Youngblood showed up on Petra's arm."

She watched as Decker closed and locked the front door. He removed his tuxedo jacket and laid it on the back of a chair.

He walked toward her, his eyes speaking volumes. "Excuse me if I don't want to talk about Youngblood right now," he said, "when all I can think about is taking that sexy red dress off you."

Desiree ran her hand down her sides, outlining her figure, luxuriating in the silken feel of the dress. "It does make me think of warm summer nights during which we make love in a white canopied bed with the French doors thrown open and a breeze fluttering the curtains."

Decker reached for her and pulled her into his arms. The look in his eyes was, frankly, dangerous. She smiled in anticipation. The man meant business tonight.

His mouth descended on hers, and he kissed her hungrily, as if he'd been thinking of nothing else all night long except this moment. What he did with his tongue was indescribable. He dipped, he tantalized. He withheld pleasure only to whip her into a sexual frenzy.

"Desi, Desiree, my desire, my goddess…" he said before lowering his head again and redoubling his efforts.

Desiree kicked off her shoes as they continued to kiss. She felt the urgent need to get naked, quickly. Decker was backing her toward the huge couch in the great room. Her legs touched the couch, and she lay down. Decker gently lowered his body onto hers, and they spent the next twenty minutes just kissing. It was like discovering the art of kissing all over again. She knew the intimate makeup of Decker's mouth, even the manner in which he breathed, how his lips tasted and felt and their unique shape. How his touch made her open up like a morning glory at the dawn of day, ready to experience everything the day would bring. She felt that way with Decker, that anything was possible as long as they were together.

As they lay there, she could feel Decker's manhood growing harder and harder until she knew his slacks must be getting tight in the crotch. The hem of her dress was hitched up to her thighs, and Decker lay between her legs. To prevent his weight from crushing her, he was holding himself up with his powerful arms. She ran her hands over his biceps, enjoying the play of corded muscles against her palms. She turned her head to the side, breaking off the kiss, breathing heavily. "Baby, let's take this upstairs."

His eyes were intoxicated when he looked down

at her. They were like a dark storm at sea. "I could kiss you all night."

"We're not teens. We know what third base feels like."

"Yeah, you're right," he said quickly, which made her laugh.

He rose and pulled her up with him. Then he picked her up and headed for the stairs. "I can walk, you know," she commented with a smile.

"When I'm too old and decrepit to carry you, then you can walk," was his reply. "Until then, I'm going to carry you."

She pretended to swoon like Scarlett O'Hara. "Oh, Rhett, you're so commanding!"

Decker laughed and ran up the remaining stairs to the landing. "Now you're showing off," Desiree said. She held on to his neck tightly. "Don't drop me."

In the bedroom, Decker set her down at the foot of the bed. He looked around. The décor was back to white, and a canopy had been added to the queen-size bed. "I'm beginning to think that scenario you dreamed up downstairs wasn't a spur-of-the-moment thought," he said.

Desiree gave him a sultry look. "I've been planning this for a couple of days. I want you naked in my white canopied bed right now."

Decker grinned and didn't waste time getting out of the rest of his tuxedo and doffing his highly shined black dress shoes.

He was naked in about thirty seconds. Desiree

had removed her dress and stood before him in a red lace bra and panties.

She could see their reflection in the bureau mirror and marveled at how well they complemented each other. Her golden-brown skin and his reddish-brown skin were a perfect match, as was their height. She fit so well in his embrace that it made her feel safe and warm and protected. She went into his arms now and sighed happily. Decker kissed the top of her head in a tender moment. Then she naughtily grasped his penis and turned her face up to his. She felt the veins along the sides filling up with blood as it rushed to manifest his lustful thoughts.

Decker reached down with both hands and cupped her behind. "Sweet cheeks, you're getting bolder and bolder."

"I've got a lot of time to make up for," she said, and pushed him onto the bed. Once she had him on his back, she straddled him and began raining kisses all down his body. She licked his nipples, enjoying it. She worked her way past his abdomen, admiring his abdominals. All the while Decker expressed his pleasure with soft moans. But when she delved farther down, he stopped her. "No, babe, if you kiss me there, I'm a goner. Then there won't be any pleasure for you until later. And I can't have that."

So he got up and playfully flipped her onto her back, grabbed a condom from the nearby nightstand drawer and rolled it onto his engorged penis. Straddling her again, he bent close to her ear and whispered, "Open up for me."

Desiree was more than willing to oblige. She eagerly spread her legs and lifted her hips off the bed as he drove home. The simple act of penetration was enough to stimulate her clitoris to such an extent she was racing toward a climax in a very short while. In the back of her mind, she wondered why she'd become so sexually responsive all of a sudden. She'd always liked having an orgasm, but with Decker the intensity seemed somehow magnified. Was it her love for him that made *making* love with him so satisfying?

Decker slowed his thrusts after she'd come the first time. Then he let her get on top once more. "This time," he said softly, "I want you to guide me inside you, concentrating on your pleasure the whole time. Close your eyes and imagine your whole body, and all of your pleasure points, being stimulated by the act of impaling yourself on me. Go ahead, try it."

Desiree got up and straddled him. Then she led him inside her and slowly lowered her body onto his until their pelvises were touching. His huge penis filled her up and rubbed enticingly against her vaginal walls, sending currents of unadulterated pleasure throughout her body. He was right. Sex was of the mind and of the body. Just that little bit of visualization helped her achieve one of the best orgasms of her life. She inwardly chided herself. She was a psychologist. She should have known all along that good sex started in the mind. Doctor or not, she had a lot to learn about making love.

After her second orgasm, Decker took over, turning her onto her back and entering her with a grateful sigh. He was so hard now that Desiree could feel veins on his penis with each mighty thrust. As the thrusts increased in frequency, she watched his face. He was smiling. Sweat had broken out across his forehead. With eyes closed and head thrust back, he came. He opened his eyes then and looked at her, and in his gray depths she saw something she could only describe as ecstasy.

He collapsed on top of her but immediately rolled onto his side beside her. They lay facing each other. He smiled at her, and Desiree smiled back. "Sleepy?" he asked.

"I don't want to go to sleep," she said. "I just want to look at you all night."

He kissed her forehead and got up. "Let me go to the bathroom, and then you can fall asleep in my arms."

Desiree watched him go with a contented smile on her lips. She felt not the slightest bit wicked enjoying the view as he walked away. That butt, those muscular legs and broad shoulders. Suddenly she got her second wind and followed him into the bathroom.

"A shower would be refreshing," she suggested with a grin.

Decker reached a hand back for her and pulled her into the shower, where for the next few minutes they enjoyed rubbing each other's bodies and generally exulting in this thing called love.

Chapter 11

Freshly showered, they returned to bed and snuggled close, not saying anything for several minutes. The room was silent except for their breathing. The only illumination was the moonlight coming through the white sheers at the windows.

Decker kissed the top of her head. "Are you sleeping?"

"No, just pensive," said Desiree.

"Want to share your thoughts with me?"

"Well, you never mentioned what it felt like when you walked into your office that day and found Yolanda sitting behind your desk."

"I was irritated," he said.

She laughed softly. "Come on, Decker, you were in love with her once. Surely you felt something more than irritation."

"I was shocked to see her there, and then her behavior quickly irritated me. She apparently thought she was going to have to seduce me to get me to go see Sawyer, so she turned on the charm, and I discovered she no longer affected me." He sighed. "It's kind of strange talking to the present woman that I'm in love with about how I feel about the woman I used to think I was in love with."

"You used to *think* you were in love with her?" Desiree asked.

"Bear with me, Dr. Gaines," he said with a chuckle. He cleared his throat, deciding that Desiree had the right to know exactly how he'd felt seeing his ex again. "Before I fell in love with you, I used to imagine a scenario that involved her begging me to take her back. I would let her sweat it out for a while, and then I would graciously give in. But I'm not the man I was five years ago. The other day, after the shock of walking into my office and finding her there wore off, the first thing I felt was irritated with her, especially when she tried to use her feminine wiles on me. How could she think that after the way she treated me, she could come back and press her body against mine and I'd do anything she asked me to?"

"She pressed her body against yours?" Desiree cried. In the darkness, he smiled at the possessiveness in her voice. That was his girl, a tigress protecting her territory.

"I didn't let her," he assured her. "Sweetness, you have nothing to worry about. I was never in love with her."

"But you said you loved her on our first date," Desiree insisted.

"I know I said I was in love with her," Decker explained, squeezing her shoulder affectionately. "But that was before I had something to compare it with. Now that I have you, I know now that what I felt for her wasn't love. She and I lived in a materialistic bubble. She was ambitious, and there's nothing wrong with that unless you don't care how you get what you crave, and she didn't. Somewhere in the back of my mind, I knew she was just using me until a better prospect came along, but I ignored it because she fit the bill for the type of woman I thought I needed on my arm in my upwardly mobile lifestyle. We were headed for disaster. I looked at her this time and realized I didn't feel anything for her. And after what she did to you back in high school, I liked her even less."

"Well, don't dislike her on my account," Desiree said with a short laugh. "I don't hate her. I feel sorry for her. I know now that bullies were often picked on themselves. Sometimes they were abused at home. Whatever her reason was for what she did, I can only thank her because I may never have developed an interest in helping others overcome mental illnesses if I hadn't been a victim. Oftentimes, some of the most productive, successful people were picked on as children. But they rose above it and didn't let that define them."

Decker squeezed her tightly. "See? That's why I love you. You can find the positive even in a hateful situation."

Desiree kissed his chin. "I'm no Miss Sunshine, but I'd rather make lemonade when life gives me lemons than be anybody's victim." She yawned. "I guess sleep just hit me in the face."

"It has been a long night," Decker said. He laughed. "Our families know how to party, don't they?"

"Yeah," Desiree said, laughing, too. "Did you see my grandpa Benjamin and Nana Mabel dancing? They put the younger couples to shame."

On Monday, Kym hesitantly knocked on Decker's office door with the news that Yolanda was there to see him. His personal assistant looked chagrined, and Decker knew it was because Yolanda had previously used her celebrity status to finagle her way into his office.

He smiled at Kym, putting her at ease. "It's all right, Kym. You can show her in."

Yolanda flounced into the room. She was dressed to the nines as usual, another designer suit, this time a deep purple skirt suit with expensive pumps. She smiled seductively at first, then, seeing that it had no effect on him, grimaced instead. Her eyes narrowed. "Decker," she said pleasantly, although Decker could have sworn he could detect a bit of venom in her tone. He wondered why.

"Yolanda," he said dryly.

"Freddy's very upset with you," she said accusingly. "He says he doesn't trust you. Why do you suppose that is, Decker?"

"I'm glad you're here, Yolanda. It saves me a phone call. I won't be taking your cousin's case. He'll have to settle for the public defender."

Her eyes narrowed menacingly. "But you said…"

"I said I'd go see him, and I did. But to be honest, he disliked me right away. You just said he was upset with me. Didn't he tell you why?"

She dismissed her cousin's opinion of him with a haughty toss of her head and said, "I'm disappointed in you, Decker. I thought you were the 'take no prisoners' type of lawyer. I guess I was wrong," she said derisively. "Or is it because what's between us isn't water under the bridge after all? Would you let an innocent man go to prison just because I broke your heart?"

Decker was determined not to lose his temper. And to be above petty name calling and vindictiveness. He simply smiled at her. "I'm sorry, but I can't help your cousin, Yolanda."

She stood there a moment, head cocked, studying him closely. Then she smiled wickedly. "Oh my God, the rumors are true!"

"Sorry?" Decker said, confused.

"We have mutual friends, Decker. Some of them tell me you're dating Desiree Gaines. I hear she's a psychologist now."

"Oh, yeah, you went to school together," Decker said casually. "She mentioned she knew you when I told her you and I used to date."

Her eyebrows rose with interest. "I bet she did."

"She said you were very nice to her. In fact, she

said if not for the wonderful way you treated her, she might not have been inspired to pursue a career in mental health."

Her eyes were cold and glittering with malice when she turned them on him. She'd obviously seen through his sarcasm. "Whatever she told you was a damned lie. I was nice to that girl, who was really pitiful in high school, by the way. She didn't know how to dress, how to style her hair. My friends and I tried to help her by offering advice."

Decker remembered Desiree's words last night about how some people who were bullies had been bullied themselves. With this thought in mind, he smiled sympathetically at Yolanda. Judging from the vicious way she was looking at him right now, she probably hadn't worked out her issues yet. "Look, Yolanda," he said, "whatever you did in high school, I'm sure you're not the same person. We all change over the years."

She held her nose in the air and gave him a condescending look. "*You* certainly have changed. For the worse! She has you wrapped around her little finger."

Decker sighed. He was trying so hard to be the type of man Desiree would be proud of. He was not going to be reduced to trading insults with this woman.

"I can't deny it," he said with a smile. "She has me completely under her control. And I've never been happier." With that, he walked over to the door and held it open for her. "Have a good life!"

"It'll never last!" she called over her shoulder and

then he heard the heels of her shoes clicking down the tiled corridor.

He smiled. She'd gotten off easy.

"I have a new friend," Madison announced during her next session with Desiree. Wearing a navy blue skirt suit and black pumps, Desiree leaned forward in her chair. The girl's face was lit from within. She looked healthier than Desiree had ever seen her, and confidence was coming off her like waves.

Madison, comfortable in jeans and a T-shirt, her sneaker-clad feet tucked under her on the couch, smiled. "Her name is Naya, and she just walked up to me one day at school and told me she believes me. Since then we've been hanging out together."

Desiree smiled happily. "That's wonderful, Madison. Is she in the same grade?"

"Naw, she's a grade ahead of me. And she's kind of popular. I think that because she's willing to be seen with me, other kids are starting to realize I'm telling the truth. Even a girl who was with the first group to approach me recently told me she was sorry for what she said."

"That's great," Desiree said. "But don't give Naya too much credit. You're the one who stood up for yourself."

"Yes, I know," Madison said. "It just feels good not to be alone at school anymore."

Desiree nodded in understanding. High school could be so alienating. It was a positive thing that

Madison had found a friend. Desiree was not about to rain on the girl's parade.

"How are you doing away from school?" she asked.

Madison smiled. "I promise you, Dr. Gaines, I'm eating and keeping it down, and I'm no longer pulling my hair out. I'm cool, really."

Desiree returned her smile. "I'm happy to hear it." The timer went off, and she looked at Madison with regret. "That went fast. We'll end here unless there's something you'd like to talk to me about that we haven't covered in the session."

Madison bounded to her feet. Desiree was pleased to see how energetic she was. "No, we've covered everything. And I'm not just saying that to be in agreement with you like I used to. I'm doing fine."

They got to their feet, and for a moment stood smiling at each other. "I never thought I'd feel so good with the secret out," Madison said frankly. "I thought telling would ruin my life, but it's only made it better."

"The truth will set you free," Desiree quoted.

"That's what my mom says," Madison said. She grabbed her shoulder bag from the couch and looked up at Desiree. "I'm making progress, huh, Dr. Gaines?"

"You are definitely making progress," Desiree said warmly.

Madison smiled at her and left. After the girl had gone, Desiree sat back down and began writing her case notes on the session. A month ago she never would have thought Madison would possess such confidence. She prayed that the prosecutor would be able to build a solid case against Sawyer. Otherwise she was afraid of the effect his release would have on Madison.

Decker's focus had always been razor sharp, which was why the firm was so successful. The lawyers, legal aides, administrative assistants and other staffers were a well-oiled machine.

He was leaving a staff meeting, heading to the courthouse with a junior partner in the firm, when his cell phone rang. Seeing that the caller was Detective Antonio Diaz, he answered immediately.

"Hello, Detective, how can I help you?"

Detective Diaz let out a satisfied sigh before saying a word. "It worked," he said with relief. "To avoid having the journal become public record, he's pleading guilty. He actually cares about his daughters and doesn't want them to ever know what's in it."

"Well, at least he cares about someone," Decker said. "Thank you, Detective."

"No, thank *you*, Mr. Riley," Detective Diaz said sincerely. "And Mrs. Sawyer, of course. If not for her he never would have pled guilty. I know his type. He would have denied his guilt until he was old and gray."

"She definitely deserves the credit. She's a very brave woman. Have you called her with the news yet?" Decker asked.

"I was just getting ready to," Detective Diaz said. When they hung up, Decker turned to his colleague. "Shall we go?"

Chapter 12

"Babe, can you take next Friday and the following Monday off from work?" Decker asked Desiree over dinner at his place one evening in late August. "I'd like to take you someplace where we can pretend the rest of the world doesn't exist for a while."

Desiree put her fork down and looked at him. They were in his kitchen, which in the months they'd been dating had changed somewhat. There was more color in it, and it no longer looked like the helm of the starship *Enterprise*. Decker had added a backsplash of redbrick tile. And the seats of the stools upon which they sat were the same deep red. "I think I can manage that," she said. "Where do you want to go?"

"We can go to the Caribbean," he suggested with

a lascivious grin. "You, in a bikini, and me, admiring you in a bikini. That's a win-win for me."

Desiree blushed, even though she thought she should have been well past the blushing stage. She and Decker knew each other's bodies as well as they knew their own. Still, whenever he looked at her as if he were undressing her with his eyes, she reacted this way. She hoped it never changed.

She was wearing a pale yellow halter-top sundress and was barefoot. Outside, the temperature was in the nineties, and a few days in the Caribbean, walking on the beach with Decker and taking dips in the ocean, sounded wonderful. But she had an even better suggestion. "The Caribbean would require flying with possible delays, plus the whole routine at the airport. Maybe we should wait until we have more days to work with to do that. What if we drove to our cabin in the mountains instead? We'd have all the privacy we want."

"You have a cabin?"

"When Lauren married Colton, she signed her cabin over to Meghan, Petra, Mina and me. She said she didn't need it, she was redecorating the cabin Colton's family owns up there. Remember, that's how they met when both of them went to the mountains to get away. It's nice up there. It has a pond stocked with trout. Plus, with Mina's lodge nearby, we get to visit family, too. Of course, there's no room service. We'd have to cook and clean for ourselves, but that's no biggie."

"Do I still get to see you in a bikini?" Decker asked. His sexy eyes lowered to her body.

"I'll bring one for each day," Desiree promised sultrily. Two could play this game.

"It's a deal," Decker said quickly, and went back to eating his dinner, not taking his eyes off her for one second. "Any chance we could skinny-dip in that pond?"

Desiree laughed. "Only at night," she said. "I'm not getting caught buck-naked in broad daylight by any uninvited guests."

Decker chuckled. "Okay, only at night." Then he stopped laughing and frowned. "Oh, I just remembered when you used the word *guests*—my parents want you to come to dinner tomorrow night. Can you make it?"

Desiree wondered why the thought of having dinner with Decker's parents caused her anxiety. She liked them, or at least, she liked June Riley. She didn't know much about Decker's dad, Thaddeus Sr., except he was one of the leading thoracic surgeons in the state. He was always nice to her when she met him at social occasions. But she'd never gotten into a conversation with him. That was probably why the thought of an entire evening with him made her nervous.

Decker smiled. "What's going on in that beautiful mind?"

"Your dad sort of intimidates me," she admitted.

"My dad intimidates lots of people. Except my mom, who's got his number, and then some. I'm not going to lie to you. He can be a tight-ass. He and my uncle Frank were polar opposites, at least where friends and family were concerned. Uncle Frank was intimidating, too, when it came to his business. But with friends and family, he was the guy you wanted to know.

"My dad had all the advantages when he was growing up, but he didn't come from people who thought they were superior to others. My grandpa Riley was a cook at a restaurant in New Orleans before he got the bright idea to come to Raleigh and start a construction company. Dad somehow felt he was raising the family's social standing by becoming a doctor. And he still feels that way. He drummed it into my head when I was a kid. Always do better than the previous generation. I know a person's position shouldn't make him feel superior to others, but I'm afraid that's how he feels.

"My mom is down-to-earth. But Dad thinks class is the be-all and end-all of his existence. Too bad he found out after he'd married my mother that she doesn't share his views." He sighed as he looked into her eyes. "I wish I didn't have to subject you to his presence. But he's my father, and family is family no matter how you sometimes wish otherwise."

Desiree sat a moment and digested Decker's words. She was aware that everyone was entitled to his own opinion, but elitism in the United States of America, in the twenty-first century, seemed ridiculous. America was a country in which, no matter where you came from, you could become anything you wanted to. She smiled at Decker. "Don't worry about it, sweetie. Your dad and I will get along just fine."

Even if he does think I'm unworthy of you, she thought.

Decker knew Desiree must be nervous about spending an evening at his parents' home on the outskirts of Raleigh, but to look at her, you would think she didn't have a nervous bone in her body. He'd told her that his father insisted on dressing for dinner, and she'd abided by his wishes by wearing a tailored white sleeveless dress with a modest bodice and a hem that came only two inches above her knees. On her feet were beige strappy sandals, and she carried a matching clutch. Her hair was in a French twist. She looked smart, sophisticated and as cool as a cucumber.

He stood in her foyer, admiring her as she playfully spun around for him. "It's summery, but I sure hope I don't spill anything on it," she said of her white dress.

Decker, wearing a suit and a tie, and highly polished black dress shoes, shook his head in appreciation. "Mmm, mmm, mmm," he said.

She laughed and moved forward to take his arm. "That's good enough for me. Let's go."

Half an hour later they were standing on the porch of the huge Victorian-style mansion. He had to school his facial expression to keep from grinning when Desiree leaned backward and gazed up at the three-story edifice. The Riley manse had been in the family for over a hundred years. It had been maintained, and improved upon, by generations of Riley men. For some reason, the males always inherited the house, and always the eldest son. His father was the eldest among his other two brothers. Uncle Frank had passed away about two years ago. His uncle Edward lived in Paris and was "in the theater," which also wasn't looked upon as a reputable calling. It was no surprise that Uncle Edward rarely came home to Raleigh except for funerals.

Wilson, the family's English butler, opened the door and said in his proper accent, "Welcome home, Master Decker. This must be Dr. Gaines. Please do come in." And he stood aside for them to enter.

"Desi," Decker said, "this is Wilson."

Desiree smiled at Wilson. Wilson was five-ten in his socks, so Desiree in those heels was taller than he was. She bent over a little when she shook his hand. "It's a pleasure to meet you, Mr. Wilson."

Looking flustered, which amused Decker, Wilson gently extracted his hand from Desiree's and said, "It's just Wilson, Dr. Gaines."

Desiree smiled warmly as she stepped into the huge black-and-white-checkered tile foyer. "Wilson it is, then." She looked around her, her eyes filled with awe. "This is some house!"

Decker had to admit, it was indeed some house. More like a museum than a house. You heard your footfalls echoing in the massive place when you walked on the hardwood and tile floors. Antiques worthy of display in the world's finest museums furnished the rooms. Decker remembered being chastised by his father for running in the house when he was a boy. "Some of these items are irreplaceable, boy. Go outside if you must behave like an animal."

Decker had spent a lot of time outdoors during his childhood.

"There you are!" cried his mother as she entered the foyer, looking lovely in an emerald-hued dress and wearing her favorite pearls. She ignored him and went straight for Desi, which he appreciated. At least one of his parents wasn't going to embarrass him tonight.

He watched the two of them hugging—tall and athletic Desiree and his petite mother, who rarely broke a sweat, unless playing bid whist with her girlfriends counted.

His mother pulled back, gazing up at Desiree with humor-lit eyes. "You're gorgeous! Welcome to our home, my dear Desi!"

Beaming, Desiree said, "Thank you. So are you. I've been looking forward to this ever since Decker told me you'd invited me. You have a beautiful home."

His mother took Desiree by the arm and led her down the hall to the library, where Decker knew his father liked to have a before-dinner drink. "This old place?" his mother said with a dismissive wave of her hand. "It's been standing for generations. I'd rather be in a condo somewhere."

Smiling, Decker followed them. "Hello, Mom, it's so good to see you, too."

His mother looked at him over her shoulder, "Oh, Decker, are you here, too? Sorry, I didn't see you. Come on, dear, you know your father's probably on his second cognac by now."

In the library, a room with all four walls covered in shelves of books, his father stood at the bay window, a glass of spirits in one hand and the other folded behind his back in a contemplative pose. He turned around when he heard them enter and grimaced. Decker knew he looked like his father. They were both tall men with large frames. Decker's features were similar to his father's, too. Photographs of him as a younger man sometimes looked uncannily like Decker today. Genetics was all they had in common. In his father, Decker saw what he would look like when he aged. But their hearts were as different as day and night.

He wondered, sometimes, if his dad got any joy out of life at all. Or, perhaps, he was perfectly happy as he was, deriving joy from the surety that he was indeed a superman in his own right.

"Thaddeus Jr.," he said, and stepped forward to shake Decker's hand, but his eyes were on Desiree. Decker shook his hand and then presented Desiree to his father in a formal manner, as was expected. "Dad, you remember Dr. Desiree Gaines, don't you?"

His father turned his head in Desiree's direction. He smiled a smile that didn't reach his eyes. "Of course, welcome to our home, Desiree."

Desiree smiled with genuine warmth. "Thank you, Dr. Riley. I'm delighted to be here."

His father gestured to a group of chairs near the fireplace, and they all sat down. Wilson, who had been standing in the back of the room, now stepped forward and asked if anyone would like a drink.

His mother asked for a sherry. Desiree said she would try a sherry, and he asked Wilson to bring him a beer in the bottle, domestic. To which his father frowned and said, "We don't buy domestic."

Decker knew that. He was just messing with his father. While they waited for their drinks, his mother said, "Desiree, I'm fascinated by your work. I've never been to a therapist before. What sort of problems do you help people with?"

Desiree turned toward his mother on the couch, visibly relaxing. Decker knew she was in her element now. "Oh, all kinds of problems," she began. "I see people who're having residual emotional problems from having been abused in some way. Married couples come to me for counseling because they're trying to save their marriages. I see people with eating disorders. I see people with phobias."

"Phobias," his mother said, obviously intrigued. "Sometimes I freak out a little when I get into an elevator—that sort of thing?"

Desiree nodded. "Many people are claustrophobic in confined places like elevators, but if it becomes an obsession, or begins to adversely affect your life, that's when you would come to see me. But a little bit of fear is to be expected. I don't like elevators, either."

His mother grinned at Desiree. Decker, having

grown up around June Riley, and thoroughly know-ing her mannerisms, knew his mother was about to ask Desiree something naughty. "Have you ever treated someone who was afraid of sex?"

"That's called erotophobia," Desiree told his mother. "Unless you're referring to the act itself, which is called genophobia. Most of the people I've treated for that had physical problems related to sex before the mental problems started manifest-ing themselves."

Decker's father cleared his throat and set his glass on the table in front of him, after which he regarded Desiree with interest. "Oh, what sort of physical problems?"

Desiree turned to him and smiled. "For example, I had a male patient who'd had open heart surgery. The doctor told him that after he was fully recov-ered, he would be able to make love to his wife. But he had an unreasoned fear of dying in her arms. It wasn't just the act of dying in her arms that terri-fied him. It was the lasting effect it would have on her after he was gone. We had to get his wife in on the therapy before we found a solution. But we did find a solution, and they're still together, still happy, and from what I hear, still happy in the bedroom."

His mother laughed. "That's wonderful. What other sorts of phobias have you treated?"

Wilson returned with their drinks and handed them around. After this was done, Desiree an-swered his mother's question. "There is a phobia for anything you can imagine. Let's start with the

A's. You've probably heard of agoraphobia, the fear of open spaces, or the fear of leaving a safe place, such as your home. I've treated several patients who suffered from that."

"I know a woman who hasn't left her house in twenty years," his mother said excitedly. She turned to his father. "You know Clare, sweetheart."

"Clare Edmonds?" asked his father incredulously. "The woman is a social gadfly. She gives the best dinner parties in Raleigh."

"Yes," his mother agreed. "But have you ever noticed her at anyone else's dinner parties?"

His father frowned, thinking. "No, as a matter of fact, I haven't."

Decker was pleased that his mother had so far been able to loosen his father up. Maybe tonight was going to be all right, after all.

"See?" said his mother. "We all lead secret lives." She looked at Desiree once more. "Go on, you're on the *A*'s."

"There's achluophobia, fear of the dark. Androphobia, fear of men. Anuptaphobia, fear of never getting married..."

"If you had androphobia, you wouldn't care about having anuptaphobia," his mother quipped, and laughed loudest at her joke.

His dad smiled his first smile of the night. "June, really, you slay me."

Desiree looked at Decker and raised her eyebrows questioningly. He wanted to tell her that was as animated as his father ever got.

"Dinner is served!" Wilson said from the doorway.

The four of them rose and went to the formal dining room, where only part of the table that could seat sixteen had been set for them.

"I told your father we could eat in the kitchen," his mother said. "But he said he wasn't entertaining in the kitchen when there was a perfectly good dining room to be had."

Decker pulled Desiree's chair out for her while his father did the same for his mother on the opposite side of the table. "I like this dining room," he said. "I can hear my echo in it."

Desiree laughed, and it was the sweetest sound to him. He bent down and kissed her cheek before sitting beside her.

As soon as they were seated, two maids came through the swinging doors into the dining room carrying silver serving platters. For the next few minutes they filled their plates with the delectable cuisine his parents' chef had prepared: Cornish game hens stuffed with savory dressing, fresh green beans sautéed with slivered almonds, spinach salad and homemade crescent rolls that melted on the tongue.

"No one's dieting tonight," his mother joked. "How do you stay so fit, Desiree? You always look so vibrant and healthy."

"Desiree has a black belt in karate," Decker said, waiting to see what his mother would do with that bit of information.

His mother put down the roll she'd been about

to bite into and laughed. "Is he joking?" she asked Desiree.

Desiree smiled modestly. "No, ma'am, he's not. But really, karate is no different from yoga or any other physical discipline. It's just something to keep me focused and in tune with my body."

"Can you beat Decker?" his mother asked with a mischievous gleam in her eye.

Desiree laughed. She met Decker's eyes across the table. "I don't know. What do you think, Decker?"

"As far as I'm concerned, you've already won," he said.

"Aw, that's so sweet," cooed his mother.

Decker's gaze moved from his mother to his father, who was cutting into his game hen and seemingly content to let his wife be the gracious hostess tonight. "Dad, how's work?"

His father sighed and put down his knife and fork as if the question had irritated him. "Decker, you know nothing much changes in surgery except the patients. I do the same thing every day, consult and operate, consult and operate. I try to stay on top of new technology, but basically surgery is surgery."

"You make it sound so fascinating," Decker said, not even trying to hide the sarcasm in his voice.

His father refused to take the bait and began eating his dinner. His mother, who over the years had learned to ignore her husband's aloofness, smiled at him and Desiree across the table. "So tell me, you two, how long has it been now since you started dating? Six months?"

"Mom, you kept up with when we started dating?" Decker asked with a grin.

"Of course, you're my only child. It's my duty to keep up with such things. I'm practicing for when I become a grandmother. Mustn't forget the little darlings' birthdays!"

"Mom, have you no shame?"

"Absolutely none," she replied happily.

He checked to see if any of his mother's nonsense was embarrassing Desiree, but she seemed unaffected by it. She was smiling and enjoying her meal, her appetite good in spite of the tension in the room. Or maybe he was imagining the tension between him and his father. Somehow he had never felt that he was good enough for his old man. Though God knew, he'd tried when he was growing up. The biggest rift came when he graduated from high school and announced he was not going to become a doctor like his father. He was interested in the law. His mother was ecstatic. Her father had been an attorney. But Thaddeus Riley Sr. railed at him and told him he had a responsibility to carry on the Riley name by becoming a physician.

"Well, since Dad doesn't want to talk about work, tell me, Mom, what have you been up to lately?" Decker asked.

His mother smiled mischievously. "Oh, managing this house is a full-time job. I keep telling your father it's much too big for the two of us. Now, if you were to get married and move in here with your bride, maybe I wouldn't feel as if this place is swallowing me up."

Decker smiled at her. "You really do have a one-track mind, don't you?"

"We're not selling the house, June," his father said between bites of game hen. "This house has been in my family for generations."

His mother ignored his father and kept her attention focused on Decker. "I always thought a cottage by the sea would be nice. That fresh salt air, walks on the beach, digging for clams," she said dreamily.

"We already own a beach house," his father put in with a narrowed look at his mother.

"Yes, but we only go there once a year," said June. "Every July. What if I wanted to go to the beach in October once in a while?"

"You know I take a month off in July," her husband said reasonably.

"That's another thing," June complained. "Maybe I'd like to vacation some other time. Have you ever thought of that?"

Decker thought his father's jaw had tightened quite a bit since his mother had started her litany about vacation time. He wondered what was really going on between his parents.

His father set his fork down and looked at his mother irritably. "June, we are not going to air our dirty laundry in public."

"We're just talking about your taking time off from work," his mother countered cheekily. "Or maybe you'd prefer a safe subject, like the weather."

She smiled at Desiree. "Lovely weather we're having, isn't it?"

Desiree returned her smile. "Just beautiful."

They continued eating their meal after that, but Decker meant to get to the bottom of this before he left tonight.

Chapter 13

After dinner, June pulled Desiree aside and whispered, "Come on, Desi, let me show you the house while the men have a little father-son time."

Desiree sent an encouraging smile Decker's way before leaving the dining room with June. She had felt the tension between Decker and his father, but as only a guest in this house, she had thought it best to ignore it and finish her meal. Whatever was brewing had probably been doing so under the surface for years.

June—for Mrs. Riley had long ago told her to call her June—led her upstairs, talking while they climbed. "Decker and his father have some issues to work through, but Tad is stoic and Decker is stubborn, so they haven't made any inroads in solving them. I suppose you sensed it." And she turned her sad brown eyes on Desiree.

"I did," Desiree confirmed, but was reluctant to say more. She spent her time listening to people and observing them. She didn't have enough information about Decker and his father's relationship to form any opinions.

When they reached the landing, June turned to the right and led her down a long hallway. They ended up in an extremely large master suite. The room was as big as Desiree's living room. There was a sitting area in the bedroom, a huge bay window overlooking the gardens, French doors leading to a balcony that was roomy enough for a table and two chairs and a chaise longue. The en suite had a Jacuzzi and separate shower and bath. Desiree looked around. "You must love soaking in that tub." It was big enough for four people.

"Some of my best thinking is done in that tub," June said as she turned away and began leading Desiree from the room. In the hallway, she turned to face Desiree, her expression grave. "Desiree, may I speak with you about something personal, and rely on you not to speak to anyone else about it?"

"Of course you can," Desiree said immediately, concerned.

"Look at me," June said.

Desiree observed her closely as she spoke. What she saw was an intelligent, attractive woman in her late fifties with an indomitable spirit. "I was twenty-four when Decker was born. I'd graduated from Spelman with a degree in English three years earlier with the intention of teaching like my mother before me. Then I met a young physician who swept me off my feet. He might not seem like it now, but Tad could turn on the charm when he wanted to. The first few years together were blissful. Then he started working sixty-hour weeks, became head of his department and began collecting countless accolades for his work.

"Don't get me wrong, I'm proud of him. But I feel like, somewhere along the way, he left me behind. What's more, I feel as though he discounts my contribution to his success. I was the woman who kept his personal life running smoothly so he could focus on being brilliant. I could overlook being invisible to him because, on occasion, he did notice me and wine me and dine me, and take me to bed and behave as if we were on our honeymoon again, but not anymore. We haven't connected as a couple in over a year."

Desiree had to make sure she understood June correctly. "When you say connected, you mean?"

"Sex, Desiree," June said in a whisper. "Do you think he has a mistress?"

Desiree almost laughed. The thought of Thaddeus Riley having a mistress was ludicrous. He had a lovely wife who put up with his taciturn behavior. No, wait, she thought, even men with understanding wives could have a chick on the side. "Are there any other indications that he might be unfaithful?"

"Like what?" asked June, whose brown eyes held an inquisitive expression.

"Like has he started paying more attention to his wardrobe, his personal hygiene? Is he taking extra showers? Has he suddenly had an interest in getting into shape? Basically, men who cheat do the same things they did to attract their wives. Having an affair also takes time and money. Does he have the extra time to spare? Have you noticed unusual charges on your cards?"

"Honey, if you only knew," June said, exasperated. "Tad and I lead separate lives in a sense. That was my suite we just left. He hasn't been in it in over a year. His suite is down the hall. So I don't know if he's taking extra showers, has been purchasing sexy underwear or anything else. Our accounts are separate. He does that to know exactly what each of us is spending, not to control the amount I spend. He's always been generous in that way. I just miss him, the man."

Then something occurred to Desiree. "The number-one reason married men of a certain age stop having sex with their wives is poor health. Do you know how his health is?"

"You would think, his being a doctor, that he would keep an eye on his health, and if there was something wrong he would tell me," June cried.

"Have you ever heard the old saying 'Doctors make the worst patients'?" Desiree asked. "I know from experience that health professionals can be the worst when it comes to monitoring their own health. They're too busy taking care of others."

"Well, I will definitely find out before the night is

done," June said. "Come on, Desi, let's go back downstairs and see what the men are up to."

"How long have you known this?" Decker asked. His heart was thudding in his chest as panic gripped him. He suddenly felt like a little boy again. He used to wonder what life would be like if he didn't have his parents. Now he might find out.

His father was standing a couple of feet away from him, swirling amber liquid in a snifter. Decker walked up and took the glass from his father's hand. "And maybe you ought to cut back on the booze while you're trying to fight cancer. Or didn't your doctor warn you about ingesting too many toxic substances?"

His father reluctantly let go of the glass. "A year, two, what difference does it make? I've done radiation treatments, and the shots that are supposed to work in conjunction with the treatments have sapped me of my manhood. If your mother knew…"

"Stop," Decker said. "Stop right there. Do you mean to tell me, you haven't told Mom anything about what you're going through?"

Thaddeus Riley Sr.'s face fell. He reached for his drink, and Decker gave it back to him. "No wonder you're bent on getting drunk," Decker said.

He turned away and began pacing the library floor while his father enjoyed his brandy. Decker couldn't believe his father had kept his illness a secret from his mother for over a year.

He faced his father again. "You've got to tell her," he insisted.

"Your mother's delicate, Decker," his father began.

Decker laughed. "Obviously you're mistaking another woman for my mother. June Riley hasn't got a delicate bone in her body. She's tough. She can handle this. What she won't be able to handle is a husband who has been lying to her for months. You'd better fess up, Dad, and now."

"Confess what?" his mother asked as she entered the library with Desiree close behind her. The two women looked at him and his father with askance expressions on their faces. The stuff was about to hit the fan, and Decker didn't plan to be in the way when it began to fly. He pointed at his father. "You have some explaining to do. Desiree and I are leaving now."

He went and kissed his mother on the cheek. "Try not to lose your cool, and just listen to him."

Then he hugged his father, even though he knew he would get a stiff hug in return. To his surprise, his father clung to him. "You open people's chests and remove their hearts for a living. Surely you can handle one tiny woman. Good luck, Dad."

Desiree said her goodbyes, as well. He watched as she gave his mother a lingering hug, as if she were trying to imbue her with some of her own strength, and then she walked up to his father and kissed him on the cheek, for which his father had the grace to look thankful for.

He grasped Desiree by the hand, and they left.

Once they were standing on the porch, he pulled Desiree into his arms and hugged her tightly. "Let's promise not to keep secrets from each other," he said as he gazed into her upturned face.

"Your dad's sick, isn't he?" she asked softly.

He nodded sadly. "He has prostate cancer, but he says the prognosis is good. He's gone through a round of radiation treatments. His doctor feels confident that it will take, but it affected his ability to have sex. He's pretty depressed about it."

"From what you said to him about his having something to explain, I take it he hasn't told your mother about his illness yet?"

"He's telling her now," Decker said as he grasped her hand again and led her down the front steps.

A week later they were on Interstate 40 en route to their mountain getaway. As Decker drove, he kept stealing glances at Desiree. This bright Friday morning, she was wearing white shorts, a simple sleeveless hot-pink V-neck shirt and white sneakers. Her hair was tied back in a ponytail, and she was bobbing her head to the beat of Aloe Blacc singing "The Man." It was one of his CDs. He was introducing her to some of his favorite artists.

She looked up and caught him watching her. He returned his attention to his driving. "When was the last time you took a few days off?" he asked.

"My sisters and I went snorkeling in the Bahamas last summer," she said.

"So about a year ago, then," Decker commented. "You, my dear, are a workaholic."

"Takes one to know one," she returned, her full lips curved in a smile. "When was the last time you went on vacation?"

"The boys and I went bass fishing last summer," he said. "I've still got fish in the freezer from that trip."

"I love bass. You didn't give me any," Desiree complained playfully. "And I don't call fishing a vacation. A vacation is when you take the time to kick back and relax. Fishing is too much work."

"That's a matter of opinion. Did you say there were trout in that pond at the cabin?"

"According to Lauren, yes," Desiree said. "But we don't fish when we go up there. We hike, ride bikes, go swimming in the pond, but no fishing."

"We should go fishing," he insisted.

"Did you bring your gear?" Desiree's smile was indulgent.

"Nope," he replied regrettably. "I wish I'd thought to bring it."

Desiree gave a tired sigh. "You can't think of everything. It's been a stressful time for both of us lately. Finally Sawyer's no longer a threat to Madison's peace of mind. She won't have to testify against him because he convicted himself. His suicide attempt was just a ploy so that his lawyer could claim insanity, but luckily the judge didn't buy it. And your parents—I'm so glad they talked things out."

Decker's hands tightened on the wheel at the mention of his parents. His dad wasn't out of the woods yet. He hadn't gotten his test results back from the tests done on him following the radiation treatments. Decker hoped that by the time he and Desiree got back to Raleigh on Monday, his dad would have heard positive news. "Yeah, on the one hand, Mom was relieved he wasn't cheating on her, but on the other, saddened that he's sick."

Desiree reached over and laid a comforting hand on his thigh. She met his gaze, hers showing staunch determination. "We've got to have faith that he's going to be all right."

Decker squeezed her hand. "I hope so because I don't want to lose my old man just when I've found him. He's opened up to me in the past week more than he has in my entire life."

"And he'll continue to open up to you. You're his son, and he loves you. Health crises tend to change people. How it'll change your father is yet to be seen, but it's a step in the right direction that he's more communicative with you and your mom."

Decker chuckled suddenly. "I forgot to tell you. He phoned Uncle Edward, his only remaining sibling. They hadn't spoken in years."

"See?" Desiree said, laughing, too. "He's coming around."

The cabin sat on ten acres of secluded land at the edge of the Great Smoky Mountains. Its only neighbor was the cabin across the pond that belonged to Colton's family. No one was occupying the Riley cabin at the moment, or so Decker had been told by Colton when he mentioned their long weekend.

They'd left Raleigh at about eight that morning and arrived at the cabin a little before noon. After he'd parked the SUV in front, Desiree got out and went to unlock the cabin's door while he retrieved their bags from the SUV's storage compartment.

Decker took a deep breath. Already the fresh mountain air was assailing his senses and making him relax. Everywhere he looked was nature's greenery. A pine forest circled the property, and the cabin had been landscaped with blue Kentucky grass. This time of year, its flowering shrubs were in bloom. It was a beautiful spot. And although the setting was definitely rustic, the cabin itself looked well kept and modern. His opinion of the cabin increased tenfold when he stepped inside. The furnishings were contemporary. There were highly polished hardwood floors, and the kitchen had every convenience, including the latest appliances and a gas range, which he loved cooking on. The air inside smelled like freshly cut lemons.

In the kitchen he noticed a vase of fresh flowers with a note leaning against it. He dropped the bags onto the kitchen floor and went to see what the note said.

Hey, Sis, I came by early this morning to air the place out and stock the fridge. Have fun you two! Mina.

He smiled. That was very sweet of her. But then,

he'd noticed that Desiree and her sisters not only loved each other; they were the best of friends.

Desiree came bounding into the kitchen with the energy of a kid. She saw him with the note in his hand. "Who's that from?"

He handed the note to her and smiled as she read it. "I'm going to call her and thank her right now. Make yourself at home, sweetie. There are two bedrooms. We're going to be in the master bedroom."

Decker assumed that was his hint to take the bags to the room they'd be using, so that was what he did. He heard Desiree already talking to Mina on her cell phone as he turned the corner and went looking for the master bedroom.

Later that day, Desiree looked up to see Decker stepping out the back door of the cabin onto the porch. She was lying on her stomach atop a chaise longue that was big enough for two, reading Walter Mosley's latest novel.

He was wearing nothing but a pair of khaki shorts, the waistband of which rode low on his hips. She put the novel down and sat up. Her skin was hot from lying in the sun in her red-and-white polka-dot bikini, but she didn't think the flush she was feeling right now could entirely be attributed to the sun.

He sat beside her. His gray gaze scanned the book's cover but did not linger. It preferred her instead, and soon was roaming from her mouth to her breasts, then farther down. He suddenly looked directly into her eyes. He didn't have to speak. He sim-

ply raised an eyebrow suggestively, and she knew
why he'd come out here.

Desiree looked around them. It was broad daylight. True, there were no other houses nearby, but
still...

She shook her head no.

He shook his head yes, and grinned.

She got up quickly, ready to bolt. He clasped her
wrist, but not hard. His touch was gentle. He rose,
too, towering over her since they were both barefoot.
She had to look up at him, which made her feel at a
disadvantage. He bent and nudged her nose with his,
testing her willingness. He brushed his lips against
hers. She blew air between full lips and kept her
gaze riveted on his. She wanted to make love, just
not outdoors. She'd never done anything so against
the norm before. What if someone drove up?

She would hear them, she decided as she threw her
head back in a gesture of surrender. Decker kissed
the hollow of her neck and worked his way down
to her breasts, burying his nose in her cleavage and
then kissing her there. Raising his head, he stood for
a moment as though gripped in indecision. Then he
grabbed the cushion off the chaise longue and put it
on the wooden planks of the porch.

This done, he got a condom out of his pocket and
dropped the foil-wrapped package onto the cushion.
He knelt on the cushion and drew her toward him.
Desiree was still not sure what he was up to, but she
was eager to see where this was going. He kissed her
belly, sending shivers of delight throughout her body.

Or maybe that was heatstroke coming on, she wasn't sure. It would serve her right for being so naughty if when she came, she fainted dead away. But for now, she was going with the flow.

He got up, unfastened her bikini top and tossed it onto the skeleton of the chaise longue, looking so naked without its cushion. Sunlight glanced off his moist reddish-brown body as he turned, abdominals ripped, to face her again. His arm muscles moved beneath taut skin when he bent and began pulling off her bikini bottoms. Still he hadn't said a word, and this added to her heightened sensibilities. The heat, the hot man undressing her, her imagination, it was all delicious.

Now that she was completely naked, he took the time to remove his shorts. He'd come with seduction in mind, apparently, because he wasn't wearing underwear. His erect penis stood at attention, ready for action. Desiree swallowed hard. She felt as if this were her first time all over again. He knelt on the cushion and pulled her down with him. Then he kissed her, and before she knew it her legs were wrapped around him with his penis caught between her stomach and his.

He was purposely not entering her since he hadn't yet put on the condom. But that hard member, hot and pulsing on her stomach, made her weak with desire. She wanted him inside her. For the moment, though, Decker was licking her nipples, undoubtedly tasting the salty sweat on her skin. He didn't seem to mind.

He was eating her as if she were a dish long craved for, but cruelly denied him, and he was ravenous.

Momentarily, he moved farther down and kissed her inner thighs, in no rush, just taking his sweet time while she arched her back, wanting him to move faster. At last, his hot tongue plunged into her feminine center, and the sensation felt so good that she moaned loudly, her voice reverberating in the Great Outdoors. It was a strange experience. They could be two wild beasts rutting in the woods.

Now the distinct smell of sex was in the air. Decker continued until she was bucking on her back in the throes of an orgasm of immense intensity. She screamed with release, the sound raw and real. Decker kissed her inner thighs until she stopped trembling; then he put on the condom and entered her. She sighed as he pushed slowly all the way inside her until they were one. In and out, and with each thrust her clitoris was achingly, lovingly stimulated. She came again, and before Decker howled that afternoon, she had ridden the wave of her pleasure three times. She lay spent in his arms, breathing heavily and supremely satisfied.

At that very moment, someone began knocking on the front door of the cabin. "Yoo-hoo, Desi, it's your grandma!"

Decker laughed. "We've got company."

Chapter 14

Mabel Brown-Beck was a woman of ample proportions in her late sixties. She had glowing brown skin with red undertones, long, thick black hair (turning grayer every day according to her), which she wore in a single braid down her back.

Desiree made the poor woman wait on the front porch until she and Decker were decent, and then she went to the door, pulled it open and cried, "Nana!" Nana was what she and her sisters had decided to call Miss Mabel after she'd married their maternal grandfather, Benjamin Beck. Their mother's mother, Benjamin's first wife, had passed away many years ago.

Mabel stepped inside wearing one of her ubiquitous pantsuits.

This one was sky blue with a sash at the waist.

She was carrying a covered dish. She handed it to Desiree. "It's my special meat loaf with mashed potatoes and sweet peas with pearl onions. You shouldn't have to prepare dinner on your first night." She looked up and beamed at Decker as if she'd just noticed him standing there. "Hello, Decker!"

Decker inclined his head respectfully, "Hello, Mrs. Beck, it's good to see you again."

Not one to rest on ceremony, Mabel hugged them both in turn, then stood back on her legs like the country woman she was and said, "I'm not going to stay." She looked at Desiree. "Your grandpa is waiting for me. It's Friday night, you know, date night."

Desiree spontaneously hugged her nana one more time and said, "Well, thank you for thinking of us, Nana. You're too sweet!"

"Oh, it was nothing, child," said Mabel modestly. "I just put you all's names in the pot while I was cooking."

Desiree smiled at the mention of the old saying, which meant that she'd cooked enough to share with her and Decker.

"Well, we appreciate it," Decker said as they walked Nana to the door. "Tell Mr. Beck hello for me."

"I will, sweetheart," Mabel assured him, and she was down the front steps and hurrying to her blue Ford F-150 pickup.

In her absence, Decker turned to Desiree, who was still holding the covered dish. He sniffed the air. "I worked up quite an appetite, and that smells delicious."

Desiree playfully held the dish out of his reach and began walking in the direction of the kitchen. "I don't know if I want to share my nana's special meat loaf with a naughty boy like you. Seducing me where anybody could walk up on us."

Decker followed her to the kitchen. "You know you liked it."

Desiree did feel hungry after making love, and she went straight to the drawer to get forks for them. They wound up eating the food right out of the dish, sitting companionably at the kitchen nook with the radio tuned to a local station.

She watched him as they consumed the food, how animated those gray eyes were, strong teeth, square jaw—the epitome of a perfect male specimen. Then she imagined him at his father's age, worn down by life, the skin around his eyes crinkled and his hair gray and possibly receding. She let that image sink in.

She loved him even more than she already had.

They polished off that delicious meal in a matter of minutes. They set their forks in the empty dish and looked at each other.

"Did I see some chocolate ice cream in the freezer?" Decker asked.

Desiree nodded happily and went to get the carton of ice cream. He knew her well.

That night, as they slept in each other's arms, the thing she dreaded most happened. She awakened with a song on her lips. To further embarrass her, it was an old hymn she remembered from childhood: "Leaning on the Everlasting Arms."

It seemed like an inappropriate choice of songs, since she was in bed with her lover at the time.

Nevertheless, the song was in her brain as she woke up, and as always, she got off a verse or two before she was able to come fully awake and control her actions.

"...Leaning, leaning, leaning on the everlasting arms...leaning, leaning, safe and secure from all alarms..."

When she was finally aware of her surroundings, she heard Decker singing with her. She opened her eyes, and he was smiling at her. "I used to like that song when the choir sang it in church," he said.

"Sorry I woke you," she said softly. "I haven't done that in a long time."

Decker reached over and switched on the lamp on the nightstand. He lay back down and gathered her in his arms. "You say you only do it when you're really happy, right?"

"Uh-huh," she murmured.

"And I, hopefully, had something to do with your happiness?"

"You had everything to do with it," she said.

"Then I'm honored. I would be happy to be awakened in the middle of the night by the sound of your singing, for the rest of my life. We harmonize pretty well together."

Desiree laughed shortly and kissed his chin. "A lesser man would have made me feel like I have a screw loose. Especially about singing that particular song while I'm naked in bed with a man I'd recently made love to. I'm stumped as to why my mind would go there."

"You do have a problem," he said. "But waking up singing isn't it."

"Then what is it?" she asked.

"You, my dear Dr. Gaines, are a sex addict."

"I am not!"

"Really?" he challenged. "Watch this."

He reached underneath the covers and cupped one of her cheeks in his big hand. Desiree squirmed, and when she moved, there he was, pressing his erection against her belly. She was instantly aroused.

"Well?" he asked smugly.

"Oh, shut up and make love to me," she said with a laugh.

The next day, right after breakfast, they packed a lunch and went for a long hike in the nearby woods. Desiree, being familiar with the area, led the way. Decker was more than willing to follow her along the narrow trails, watching her hips sway in her short shorts. They were both dressed in shorts, T-shirts and hiking boots, and carrying backpacks. Desiree had brought a walking stick, an item she told him her grandfather had turned her on to when she was a kid. The walking stick had many uses, according to Mr. Beck. You could lean on it when you tired out. It was great for pushing aside bushes and low-hanging branches on trees. And, God forbid, if you ran into a wild animal, or worse, a rattlesnake, it just might save your life.

Desiree looked back at him as they crested a hill. "We're almost at that ridge I was telling you about. From there you'll be able to see for miles. This area is so beautiful in the warm months. Wintertime can be harsh. Folks can get snowed in and be cut off from the rest of the county because they're so isolated."

At the ridge they stood at the summit, and could indeed see the entire area, how the colors of the trees changed with each individual copse. Desiree pointed to various sections. "That's pine," she said. "And that's sugar maple."

Decker couldn't tell one tree from another. He was a city boy. His father had never taken him fishing or hunting or camping. But he could appreciate the forest's aesthetic beauty.

He was a little distracted right now, though, because he was waiting for the right moment to say something to Desiree. They had been walking for a couple of hours, and now seemed as good a time as any.

"Desi, can we sit for a while?"

She turned concerned eyes on him. "Sure," she said. "We can take a rest here."

She took a long, thick towel from her backpack and spread it on the sparse grass atop the hill. Decker removed his backpack and sat down beside her on the towel. They sat with their knees drawn up and looked out over the valley for a few minutes without speaking.

He was the one to break the silence. "Are you still wondering why you woke up singing that hymn early this morning?"

She smiled at him and shrugged. "The brain is a mystery."

"Is it really such a mystery?" he said. "Maybe your mind was telling you that you are safe and secure in my arms, Desi, that you can count on me to be there for you."

She met his gaze, her own contemplative, and he knew she was analyzing his theory in her mind. She smiled. "I know I can count on you."

"Do you really?" he asked as he reached into his shorts pocket and retrieved a ten-carat emerald surrounded by white diamonds, a ring his mother had given him. It had belonged to his great-grandmother, Constance Riley, and had been passed down in his family for three generations. He would be the fourth Riley man to present it to the woman he loved when he asked her to marry him.

The shock on Desiree's face was almost comical. Her beautiful eyes stretched, and she covered her mouth with a hand, as if that would keep her from screaming aloud. Then she gave a strangled gasp and cried, "Oh, my God, are you asking me to marry you?"

He briefly looked up at the clear, blue sky, and then returned his gaze to hers. "While God is watching, yes, Desiree, I'm asking you to be my wife," he said with a smile. "I have been lifted by your love. You make me want to be a better man. I know what I want. I know who I want. I spent so much of my life thinking that material things mattered. But I know now that the greatest thing you can have in your life, the thing that brings true happiness, is love. I scoffed at love, saying I was happier without the responsibilities that came with it, but I was just fooling myself. Desiree, will you marry me and let me love you for the rest of our lives?"

She burst into tears and threw her arms around his neck. "Yes, yes, I'll marry you."

He slipped the ring onto her trembling hand. Then he kissed her through her tears. When they parted, she looked down at the ring on her finger. "It's beautiful."

He told her the history of the ring, and she started crying all over again. "That's a beautiful tradition," she breathed. "I'm honored to be a part of it."

His heart was so full of love at that point he felt close to tears himself when he said, "No, I'm the one who's honored that you accepted me."

They sat there on that ridge for several minutes, hugging each other tightly, sighing with contentment. It was the happiest day of his life.

Going back to work on Tuesday morning, after a glorious long weekend with Decker, was a shock to Desiree's system. She didn't want to let go of the effects of the almost surreal time she'd spent with him in the mountains. And she caught herself gazing at her ring at the oddest moments: while she should have been listening intently to a patient during a session, or while driving, which could have proven disastrous.

Once they announced their engagement to friends and family, time seemed to speed up. Her mother and sisters especially began peppering her with questions. When was the wedding? Where would it be held? Had she given any thought to a dress, the reception, the honeymoon? Her head was spinning.

One night when Decker came over to dinner, she told him about it and asked him as they sat across from each other in the dining room, "Have you ever considered eloping?"

He laughed shortly. He looked handsome in a baby-blue short-sleeve pullover shirt and dark blue jeans. "Isn't that supposed to be the groom's question to the bride? I thought girls loved planning their dream wedding."

"As you probably know by now, I'm not a normal girl," she said with a smile. "I'm okay with breaking the rules. The way I look at it, a big wedding is a prelude to the real thing, which is marriage itself. Why do couples have a wedding, anyway? For their friends and family," she theorized.

"They also do it for the memories," Decker reasoned. "My mom still brings out her wedding album and relives that day. Do you want our children to look at wedding pictures of us at a Las Vegas chapel?"

Desiree rolled her eyes at the notion. "To each his own, but no, I'd rather have friends and family in our pictures."

"Then it's a wedding," Decker said with finality.

* * *

Between the two families, the guest list quickly increased to two hundred people. Finding a venue for that number proved quite easy when Decker's parents offered their mansion and its gardens as the perfect spot. Desiree was aided in making plans by three key women: her mother, Virginia, Decker's mother, June, and his aunt Veronica, who was also a close friend of Desiree's. Plus, Desiree hired Evan Rivera, the significant other of her karate partner, John Tanaka, to coordinate everything. Evan was a wedding planner.

Their expertise in social matters freed Desiree and her sisters up to prepare her for her big day. All four of her sisters were supporting her in this because Petra had come from New York, where she'd moved in order to begin work on the reality show she'd finally agreed to do in spite of her apparent dislike for the network's owner, Chance Youngblood.

And Decker had personally phoned his uncle Edward in Paris to invite him to the wedding. He was surprised, and very pleased, when Uncle Edward said he wouldn't miss it for the world.

Desiree's wedding dress was a vintage pale pink Carolina Herrera sheath. The color looked like ivory tinged with pink. The material had a matte finish, and was so soft that when she put the dress on, it flowed down her body like silk. Sleeveless with a scoop neck that revealed a hint of cleavage, it had a six-foot train. Her sisters, her bridesmaids and matrons of honor were attired in deep pink dresses in various styles that enhanced each of their figures. Desiree stood in front of the mirror in June's huge suite. Her mother, sisters, June and Veronica were there making sure she stayed cool, calm and collected.

"I don't think I've ever seen a pink wedding gown before," her mother commented, her eyes assessing her daughter. "But I like it!"

"It's not really pink," Desiree said, smiling at her reflection. "It's kind of like a white rose, blushing."

Her mother responded by coming to her and adjusting a lock of hair that had fallen in her face. Virginia had done her hair in an upswept style, something that was now an established tradition for a Gaines sister wedding.

"Well, I love it," Mina said, moving forward to gently touch Desiree on the back. Desiree smiled at her sister, who had a protective hand on her baby bump.

"Yeah, it really brings out your skin tone," Meghan put in.

"Of course, you're not going to be wearing it long after Decker gets you alone after the wedding," Lauren said. She had left Colton Jr. with his father today. Colton was somewhere down the hall in another bedroom, helping Decker prepare for his starring role as groom.

"You know, Desi, you don't have to fall for this archaic tradition of proclaiming your love before friends and family called a wedding. You and Decker would be just as married if you just lived together."

"Petra!" every other female in the room cried.

Desiree just smiled at her sister. "I know, sis, we're just doing it so that the children won't be illegitimate."

"And speaking of illegitimate children," Petra went on. "What makes a child legitimate? Jesus—"

"Stop right there," their mother exclaimed. "If you say our Lord Jesus Christ was illegitimate, I'm going to put you over my knee, and don't think I can't do it!"

There was a knock at the door. It was Evan, the wedding coordinator, coming to say it was time for the bride to go downstairs.

Desiree was glad for the interruption. She figured Petra was going to incite a fistfight with her revolutionary views on marriage if they didn't get this show on the road soon.

Besides, she couldn't wait to see Decker, whom she hadn't seen in twenty-four hours. She knew the sight of him was going to make her burst into tears of happiness.

"You're two minutes from being a married man," Colton joked as he and Decker approached the raised platform in the rose garden, where the minister already stood waiting. "You can still run, if you want to."

"I would fire you as best man if I had time to get a replacement," Decker returned, grinning. He wasn't in the least bit nervous. He'd been looking forward to this day for a long time. Soon they were standing near the minister on the platform, and Decker said, "Check your pockets for the ring."

Colton dutifully patted his coat's pocket. "Don't worry, I've got you covered."

The wedding processional began, and Decker looked up to see a sweet little girl tossing rose petals on the white runner, followed by Desiree's sisters on the arms of groomsmen.

When he glimpsed Desiree strolling down the aisle on her father's arm, his heart filled with joy. He sighed. She looked like an angel. The dress was something else. It fit her body as though it had been poured over her, and lent just the right amount of sophistication to her impeccable style. But it was the expression in her eyes that thrilled him the most. Apart from her appearance, she possessed a depth of character that was incomparable. He knew he had in her a woman who would not crumble in the wake of whatever troubles life threw their way. He would try his best to be worthy of such a woman.

Her father placed her hand in his and went to take his seat as the minister intoned, "We are gathered here today to unite in holy matrimony…"

It was hard for Decker to concentrate on the minister's words when his love, his life and his soon-to-be wife was looking up at him with such naked passion. He couldn't help it; he pulled her into his arms, squashing her chest against his and bent and planted a kiss on her lips. She sighed and wrapped her arms around his neck. The kiss deepened, and everything else faded out of existence for him.

He thought he heard the minister say, "We haven't gotten to that part yet, son!" But he could have been mistaken. He was too busy kissing his bride.

It was his father who walked up onto the raised platform, put a firm hand on his shoulder and said, "Thaddeus Jr., you're embarrassing the family. Let go of the girl long enough to marry her!"

Decker came to his senses and released Desiree, who was looking up at him with a dazed, yet pleasant, expression in her beautiful eyes. "Oh, sorry," he murmured.

The guests laughed good-naturedly, after which the minister cleared his throat and began the ceremony.

Decker peered into Desiree's eyes as the minister continued.

"I hope I didn't embarrass you," he whispered to her.

She smiled. "If that's how you embarrass me, you can do it again in a few minutes."

Vows were said. Rings were placed on fingers. Then the minister beamed at them and said, "I now pronounce you husband and wife. *Now* you may kiss your bride, son!"

Decker bent and kissed Desiree long and passionately. The guests got to their feet, applauding, laughing uproariously and in general celebrating the love they were witnessing at this moment. Music filled the air: John Legend singing "All of Me."

Momentarily, Decker picked up his bride and carried her back down the aisle and inside the mansion to the ballroom, where the reception would be held.

A few minutes later, they were dancing their first dance to "These Arms of Mine" by Otis Redding.

He couldn't take his eyes off his wife, his lover, his best friend. She'd never looked more beautiful to him. She glowed as if she'd been infused with an angelic light.

"I can't believe we're finally here after all this time," he said softly in her ear. "I never thought I'd be lucky enough to win your heart."

Desiree looked him deeply in the eyes and murmured, "You didn't win it, you stole it right out from under me. You've taught me what it really means to be in love."

After that statement, the only thing Decker could think to do was kiss his bride with every ounce of passion in him.

And so he did.

* * * * *

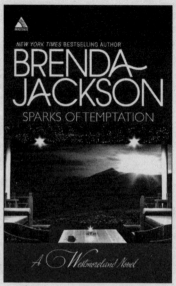

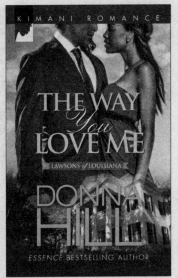

REQUEST YOUR FREE BOOKS!

2 FREE NOVELS PLUS 2 FREE GIFTS!

KIMANI™
ROMANCE

Love's ultimate destination!

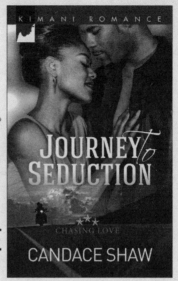